Steven Reitz

About the Author

Suicide's Girlfriend is ELIZABETH EVANS's fifth book.
The recipient of numerous awards for her writing,
Evans makes her home in Tucson, Arizona.

ALSO BY ELIZABETH EVANS

The Blue Hour
Carter Clay
Rowing in Eden
Locomotion

SUICIDE'S
girlfriend

A Novella and Short Stories

ELIZABETH EVANS

Perennial

An Imprint of HarperCollinsPublishers

HarperCollins books may be purchased for educational, business, or sales promotional use. For information, please e-mail the Special Markets Department at SPsales@harpercollins.com.

FIRST EDITION

Designed by Jamie Kerner-Scott

Library of Congress Cataloging-in-Publication Data is available.

ISBN 0-06-095467-1

14 15 16 ❖/RRD 10 9 8 7 6 5 4 3

These Stories Have Appeared in the Following Publications

"Ransom," in
American Fiction

"Americans," in
Crazyhorse

"Beautiful Land," in
Sonora Review

"Thieves," in
Crazyhorse

"English as a Second Language," in
Crazyhorse

"Home Ec," in
Zone

"Blood and Gore," in
The Quarterly

"Voodoo Girls on Ice," in
American Fiction

"A New Life," in
Prairie Schooner

"Americans" also appears in the anthology
The Best of Crazyhorse (1990).

ACKNOWLEDGMENTS

Special thanks to the Centrum Foundation, Port Townsend, Washington, and the Barbara Deming Memorial Fund, Brooklyn, New York, for their support of this project.

CONTENTS

Suicide's
Girlfriend

Ransom

"THERE DAD COMES," Mickey whispered.

"Wait," I said, "wait." Because it was still far off, the car looked small and dark, but it grew lighter, a dusty blue. Dad. Slipping off the road and into the wide ditch along the highway, then rolling back up again, so slow that from where we kids stood the motion looked almost peaceful, like an ocean wave.

I tucked little Krystal higher up on my shoulder and prayed she'd go on sleeping. "Knock that off now," I told the rest. Except for Mickey, they'd all started throwing gravel from the shoulder as soon as we left the truck stop. Their cheeks were red with the cold, but they still laughed, they tumbled into the ditch on purpose. They didn't know what was what.

A big truck went by, fast enough that it sucked at our clothes and made things even colder. When the trucker got close to dangerous Dad's car, he leaned on the horn.

"Wow," Mickey said. He squinted down the road. "Dad's driving doesn't look so hot."

"When's it ever?" I asked. The rate Dad came on, we'd still be standing on the side of the highway when spring arrived; by the time he got there, maybe the climate would have changed entirely, Nebraska would be under the sea again and the kids and I would all have flippers.

"What sort of mood do you figure he's in now?" Mickey asked.

"Ha," I said. I knew Mickey wanted to blame me for us being out here, but it had been Mickey that Dad was burned at *yesterday*, so mad he punched a hole in the bathroom. Dad hadn't even yet fixed the hole he kicked between the living room and the hall last summer. *That* particular hole. The little ones liked to look at each other through that hole. Sammy's idea of a good time: pull a diaper box out in the hall and sit there watching TV through the hole. Personally, the hole made me sick: always plaster dust on the floor from the little kids picking, and the wall smudged with finger marks.

I cried at the new hole, but when Dad said, "Stop your blubbering," I did. I wanted to be strong. I wanted to provide the children with a lifelong model of Christian tolerance—which, if I didn't have, I didn't have a thing. Except maybe the children. Maybe Krystal, now shifting in my arms on that cold and dirty road that her father traveled down slow as a camel, slower.

I blew into the yellow down of Krystal's hair, made a star. If Krystal looked like anybody on earth, I was it. No one alive would have guessed such a perfect child came from Dad and my stepmother, Anndean. But that's always the way with children, isn't it? When my real mom brought home my brothers and sisters from the hospital, they smelled sweet as bread. They might have cried out for relief of earthly suffering, but they never did a truly bad or cruel thing to anybody.

"Whoa!" Mickey threw his hands up before him like somebody opening a sheet onto a bed. I looked. Dad's car climbed the median, it headed straight for a big pole.

The children screamed. They didn't even know what had happened. They screamed because I did, and they were hooked to me that way, like those Christmas tree lights where if one goes out they all do. Still, Dad missed the pole. He stuck his head out the window, like he'd just found the right address, any moment someone would call out, "Come on in for a beer, Gary!"

Mickey started toward Dad, but I said, "Wait. We wait til *he* comes for us. He can do that at least."

"But I'm *cold*, Marie."

"Of course you're cold," I told him. "It's cold out here. If you weren't cold, something would be wrong with you, so I guess you're all right."

Mickey smiled. I could always make him smile. I smiled back to help him along, but I didn't feel like smiling. I wished we were in the truck-stop diner still. Krystal would wake soon, and then what? I'd used the last diapers and bottles over two hours ago; the three littlest kids were sure to be wet by now, and pretty soon they'd notice, start to holler.

I breathed on Krystal's face to warm it. The most wonderful baby in the world—like all babies—she remained as yet unspoiled by contact with us, but I imagined her in our company, simmering like a poor little pot roast until she, too, cooked clear through.

Dad started to work on backing up off the median. I asked Mickey, "If Dad died right now, do you think he'd go to heaven?"

"Don't start," Mickey said, "that's how we got here in the first place, Marie."

I sniffed. The sound frightened me. I looked around for Anndean. Then I did it again: sniff!

"Did you hear that, Mickey?" I said. "Did you hear me sniff?"

"Don't change the subject," Mickey said. "It *is* your fault, Marie."

"I've been infected with Anndean's gruesome habit!" I cried. "She's infected me, Mickey!"

Mickey didn't smile. Because of this morning. Anndean had wanted her coffee, but it still perked, so since I couldn't bring her a cup yet, I just sat down with her and the children at the breakfast table. Anndean turned away from the TV to give me a dose of her fishy stare. That's what got me started. And the sniff. As always, she sniffed: sniff, like she understood things through her nose, or else I stunk. Anndean wasn't that much older than me, and I was smarter, but marriage to Dad gave her the advantage, say, a sledgehammer has over something like a microscope or a fancy computer: whatever I could do, she could put an end to it, quick.

"You!" she said, and wagged her cigarette beneath my nose. "Stop looking, you!"

"Did I look?" I said. "I didn't mean to, Anndean, but I suppose observation is my nature." This was not a lie. "You're a good observer," more than one teacher at the schools had told me. Indeed, I often found myself fascinated by the bottom line of Anndean's face, which traveled from ear to ear by the shortest distance, so that, head-on, Anndean looked like a mailbox we had the time we lived in the country.

Judge not lest ye be judged, but I did suspect that the *inside* of Anndean's head was like the mailbox, too; maybe once a day something ended up in there, but she mostly stood empty. A sweeter, more practical woman would have let us use the space between her ears for storing some of the stuff that spilled out of cupboards and closets and boxes wherever we lived. Canned goods, I thought once, just to make myself laugh, canned goods would be my choice.

"Anndean," I had said this morning. I turned down the TV despite the honking of the children. "Do you know, Anndean, I used to think and think, Why are we saved by the coming of Jesus? A visit's a visit. Rules are rules, okay, but how does following them give us eternal life? How could Jesus die for *our* sins? And in so doing ransom us all from eternal death?"

Anndean flicked at my ear with her fingernails to keep me from getting close. Anndean—she was nothing like my real mother. My real mother looked precisely like the movie star Susan Sarandon, except she had blue eyes. She *never* hurt us kids and it upset her so when Dad did that she had to go in her room and just lock the door. Anndean, on the other hand, could always be counted on to possess, within easy reach, a pointed shoe, a serving fork, some item that would let her join the fray.

She didn't want to listen this morning, but I went on: "Then I figured it out. Even though God made men, He couldn't understand what it meant to be a man until He took the form of man. And when He did! And saw how bad life was! How it pretty much stunk most of the time, and people did *lousy* things to one another, sometimes not even out of the rottenness of their hearts, but because He gave them bad equipment . . . why, He put His face in His hands. He just said, 'I don't blame anybody for anything!' Which was all He *could* say, really, since it was His fault, but, let's face it, the rest of us don't always behave that graciously."

I did not look directly at Anndean, but I watched for signs of absorption. Like I said, she was not bright. She thought TV programs where people sat in chairs and discussed things like wars and the national debt—I could *see* Anndean thought that those shows appeared by mistake, that she caught glimpses of them the way she might spy strangers in hospital rooms while on her way to visit a friend. "Turn!" she'd say if I stopped to hear a little, "Turn, turn, turn!"

If my theory about Jesus relieved Anndean this morning, she did not let on. Maybe she accepted God's forgiveness as her due, though she *had* served time for breaking and entering, *and* forgery, *and* when my baby was born one month after her Krystal—Tommy Lawrence Handsell I named him, though nobody cared, the people who adopted him gave him a name I will never know as long as I live—when my baby was born Anndean worked hard and long to persuade Dad I had to give him away.

"Anndean," I said, "forgiveness and forbearance." She turned the TV back up, lit another cigarette, stubbed out the last in her jam. "Even," I told her, "for Jesus, who made the fig tree *wither* when He was hungry and it bore no fruit!"

Anndean looked around the room at all those children waiting to be fed. She'd given her Krystal a bottle all right, she did care for Krystal. Right then, she reached over and stuck her finger under Krystal's sleeper and gave her a little tickle. Then she looked at me. Ran her fingers down her neck and into the V of her bathrobe. Rose from her chair. Opened her mouth.

"Get out of my house!" she yelled. She chased me into the living room with the coffeepot, throwing coffee toward me like I was moving fire, and screaming, and whacking Erin in the face with Krystal's bottle. "Out!"

While she screamed Dad out of bed, I helped the little kids find something to put on, and grabbed up diapers and things. I couldn't locate a shirt so I just stuffed my nightgown in my jeans. Krystal lay on my bunk, bawling; but once I picked her up, she'd be fine. I'd been more mother to her than Anndean any day of the week. I'd meant to breast nurse Tommy so he'd have all the protection possible against whatever was out there, and when they took him away, I secretly gave the milk to Krystal, twice a day for a whole month, once for her night feeding and again before the rest got up.

"Out!" screamed Anndean. "Out!"

When Dad and us started off down the drive, she came after. She threw toys and chunks of snow at the car. A couple of neighbors stuck their heads out to look. I think that's when it occurred to Anndean that I had Krystal. "Bring back my baby!" she yelled.

Dad looked in the rearview mirror, then over at me and Krystal. His hair was mashed with sleep. He looked like he had a fry pan stuck on his head. "Think I ought to give her a chance to cool off?" he said.

Chances were, if I agreed with him, he'd get suspicious. He'd stop the car and take Krystal back. So I kept my mouth shut. And prayed. For nothing more than forbearance and forgiveness. But I suspected my prayers concealed wishes, had little pockets sly as those folds in your brain scientists say contain everything you ever heard or said or smelled, even though you don't know it.

With Krystal in my lap, maybe I secretly prayed for all the things that would give me the peace I seemed to need before I got forbearance. Like an automobile safety seat for Krystal. And knowing my Tommy was safe and sound. And revenge on Dad and Anndean.

The way Anndean acted about my theory, you'd have thought I came up with it for my own pleasure. But consider this: If everybody *did* go to heaven, heaven would just be life on earth all over again, wouldn't it? Also, suppose you're nuts and kill somebody. Suppose you're not and do the same. Does that mean you are nuts?

The children had shivered and shook in the car this morning. I'd tried to comfort them. I'd put my foot over the rusted-out place in the floor to keep splatters of slush from shooting up at us. If the rusted-out place had been there two years ago, January 17, maybe Mom could not have killed herself. I've tortured and tortured myself, trying to rust out the metal earlier or make one of the windows impossible to roll tight. I didn't ever want to get in a car again after that. I thought we ought to become Amish. The Amish don't have cars. They live in solid houses where if a thing wears out, they fix it, or make another. They only have things they *can* fix. They grow their food. They eat hot meals with crowds of people who pray and believe the same things, so at least you had a chance of turning out right for your earthly life, and didn't just figure you'd say "sorry" before you died.

This morning, when Dad dropped us at that truck stop—a place out farther than I could remember ever going before—he just said, "Get something to eat. I'll be by later. You watch for me."

He knew I didn't have any money, so why ask him for some? Off he drove, and there stood the kids, six of them besides me and the baby, waiting to eat.

"May as well get whatever you want," I told them; and the waitress: "Our dad'll be by later."

Of course, I could not entirely stop the kids from spilling syrup and tearing open sugars and blowing straws. I scolded, I prayed, but our waitress still had to stand a couple feet from the table to get our dessert orders. "But which dessert's *best*?" Sammy cried. "Which one's very *best*, Marie?"

"Sorry," I told the waitress. She deserved it. She had forbearance, like my real mom. A skinny man at the counter asked her if he could have "a beaver on rye," and she didn't frown or smile or anything. I really admired her until about eleven thirty, at which time she began to cast looks my way, like, "Where's your dad?" and "So who's paying for all this?"

I stared out the window at all those trucks. I thought, I will be stuck in this booth the rest of my life and I've already been here forever.

"Say, darling, you watching for your boyfriend?"

This came from a trucker across the way. Sweet-voiced. That sliver of face I allowed in my sight not entirely bad. In self-defense, I began to pray, "Lead us not into temptation . . . ," but found I could not hold on, both prayer and temptation spun on the same globe, their edges blurred like the borders between countries.

"Psst! You in the nightgown!"

"That man wants you, Marie!" the children cried. "Marie! Marie, look!"

"Marie!" said the trucker. "Look!"

I looked. A dinner plate held up, and on its chopped steak, the words "I love you" unwound in bright red catsup.

"Hey!" protested the trucker as an enormous man in a blue windbreaker came between me and my view of the trucker's plate.

"Chuck Rappenhoe's the name," said the man in the windbreaker.

At my mom's funeral, I met my granddad. I suppose Mr. Rappenhoe was about his age, with the same kind of gray hair—it looked like it'd been chipped at with a chisel. Mr. Rappenhoe wore glasses. He had a gap-toothed smile, like a jack-o'-lantern; but he frowned at my trucker, who just laughed and started eating the chopped steak.

"Don't pay any mind to that joker," Mr. Rappenhoe said, then asked if he could sit with us a while.

I regretted the loss of the trucker, but maybe Mr. Rappenhoe was my reluctant prayer made flesh. Maybe he'd pick up our tab.

"That's a beautiful baby," said Mr. Rappenhoe. "Is that your baby, young lady?"

The children had seen me go around big as a house, but they giggled as if his question were something silly. I glared them down. They knew from Social Service calls not to correct me when I looked that way. "Yeah, she's mine," I said.

Mr. Rappenhoe put one of his big fingers in Krystal's hand. Bang, she leaned over and bit him, hard, with those sharp little teeth of hers.

"Yikes," Mr. Rappenhoe said, but then just grinned. He acted as if he didn't even notice that, under our coats, both Theresa and me wore nightgowns or that Erin's eye was turning black and there was jam in his hair.

"I came here to study radio electronics," he said. "Me and my wife farm, but, on the side, I've always been good at fixing things."

Of course, it crosses any person's mind that such a man might be a mass murderer/child rapist in disguise, but Krystal liked him, all the children liked him. While Sammy combed, this way and that, Mr. Rappenhoe's old gray hair, Mr. Rappenhoe smiled and explained that just that morning he had finished his final exam, so he'd come over here to celebrate with a piece of pie.

I didn't hear all of what he said because over by the cash register, my trucker was giving me a sign: "Tonight." Pointed his finger at me like we were a regular thing. "You be here." It gave me shivers. Was he handsome? Ugly? I watched him cross the lot and swing himself into a big blue truck, but I couldn't tell a thing. Everything needed further investigation.

Mr. Rappenhoe frowned while he worked to untangle a snarl in Theresa's hair, but he sounded happy: "Tomorrow, bright and early, *adieu* to the Three Bells Motel! I load the car and head on home to Arkansas!" He stuck his comb in his back pocket and smiled. He creased his napkin with his thumbnail, made a shy boy's face. "I missed the wife so a couple times I drove home in the middle of the night just to eat breakfast with her!"

He showed us her photograph. "She seems nice all right," I said. I knew they couldn't be Amish since he'd mentioned a car and electronics. Still . . . farmers, and one of them knew how to fix things!

"How many kids you got?" Mickey asked.

Mr. Rappenhoe shook his head. "We kept trying, but just weren't blessed. Turns out now we're too old to adopt." He patted Krystal's cheek. She had taken charge of his glasses by then. She worked the hinges back and forth like she meant to snap the bows right off. "Look at that," Mr. Rappenhoe said, "she's a smart one, isn't she?"

Who could answer? Here sat the best dad I ever met, without even one child to be dad to! It just showed, again, the rightness of my theory, and so I said.

Mr. Rappenhoe listened, but then *he* said, as if he put away my theory entirely, "Christ came to ask us to be better. Maybe we're home free in the end, Marie, but he still asked us to be better."

The waitress stopped by the table, rag squashed in her hand, face all red. "These kids have sat here over four hours and I take it you aren't the dad?" she said to Mr. Rappenhoe.

I blushed. All the children old enough to know beans blushed. "He'll be here," I said. After she left, I told Mr. Rappenhoe, "I try to do everything Jesus told the Rich Young Ruler, but even Jesus didn't honor His parents. Jesus said He didn't even have a family! If my father had been better to my mother . . ." I didn't want to tell Mr. Rappenhoe what Mom did, so I backed up a little. "If he were nice to her, she'd be happier."

Mr. Rappenhoe nodded. He looked serious, but not mad, like the counselor they had me talk to when I got pregnant.

A few minutes after he had left, the waitress came over. "Old pumpkin head paid for you," she had said. Sniff. And turned on her fat white heel.

~

After Dad finally got down off the median, and all of us were in the car, he gave me one of his biggest, booziest smiles. I knew this meant he was headed for tears, about Mom, and every bad deal he ever met, and how we didn't appreciate him. He sort of sloshed the car off the road, barely missed the sandwich board in the truck-stop yard: $1.13 Reg. It was my hand on the wheel that got us back on the road just as the station manager ran out.

Dad says to me: "Anndean didn't mean nothing this morning, Marie. Why, you kids are all we got!"

I thought about that. Was that true? "Still," I said, "Tommy was all I got. Had." I wiped the wet off the windshield. Put the bunch of us together in a car and it dripped like a covered pot. I said, "Thou shalt not steal, Dad."

"Oh, hell." Dad rested his chin on the steering wheel. He squinted at the winter afternoon as if it were a terrible storm and he were the sea captain. "First one to spot a church gets a quarter," he said, "and no more lip from you, Marie."

~

The secretary lady at St. John's Episcopal saw Dad drop us off. She seemed embarrassed for us, but she must have had similar cases in the past since she knew what to do. Right away she got a box of graham crackers from a Sunday school classroom, and, by five thirty, the kids and I were eating lasagna and something called green beans amandine at the home of a church family named Zenor. Dry pants for the little ones. A whole case of Krystal's favorite formula on the kitchen counter.

"Quiet down!" I told the kids. The Zenor house knocked them out: toys in the basement, more in the bedrooms, a place just for finger painting and clay and puzzles, a clothes chute to holler down, the boy's bed topped by a frame so it looked like an outdoors tent. Everybody kept jumping out of their chairs to go see this or that. Nuts—even Mickey, who should've remembered other times that weren't so different—as if we might live in that nice house with candles on the table forever.

I knew better. Dad might not come tomorrow, but he'd be back the day after tomorrow for sure. You couldn't understand why, but he would. "Trouble with the oldest," he'd tell Social Service. "You know she's trouble."

While I dished myself seconds of the lasagna, I tried on the idea of me running off with all the kids in the back of that trucker's trailer.

Then I tried just Krystal, me, and the trucker. I kept it simple, but it didn't look good, either way.

"Mrs. Zenor," I said, when Mr. Zenor got up to get us more milk— Mrs. Zenor was pretty and nice like some schoolteachers I'd had— "what's a person have to do to be a nun?"

"We're not Catholics!" cried her son and daughter. Them, I didn't like. Them, I gave a look. Not that they noticed. They kept on eating, chewing up their little mouthfuls of food like they had all the time in the world.

"I'm not Catholic either," I told Mrs. Zenor, "I just wondered."

Mrs. Zenor nodded. She tilted her head to one side: "Let's see if I can get all your names right!" she said.

Chuck Rappenhoe couldn't *believe* himself so lucky as to set Theresa or Krystal on his knee, while Mrs. Zenor couldn't believe anybody would ask her to return the children she fancied. She and Mr. Zenor looked across their shiny table at each other with a crazy kind of happiness. Later on, while the bigger kids ran around the house and I watched TV with the little ones, I heard her on the telephone:

"This Krystal's a darling, Kim! And I can just imagine your Glenn with a little brother . . ."

Mrs. Zenor was a good woman, but misguided. She thought taking one or two of the children would be like picking out a pair of hamsters, easy, she'd tuck them into a spare corner, and their gratitude would shape them into something better than what she already had. By about nine-thirty, however, she began to see the error of her ways. She came downstairs in her bathrobe. Without makeup she looked older, tired. I felt old and tired myself. I propped Krystal with her bottle and the three of us watched the end of a show called *The Exterminator*.

Now and then Mrs. Zenor looked up at the ceiling. "Do you usually just let them run down?" she asked me. Thud, went children jumping off beds. "I kissed them good night at about nine, but in five minutes, they all were up again."

Probably, they started arguing about who she kissed first and why and if she liked one of them more than the others. What if she thought she had to kiss me, too? Except for the children, and the person who was Tommy's dad, nobody had kissed me since Mom died.

I told her, "You may blame me that they're not better mannered, but we've been subject to bad influences."

Mrs. Zenor smiled. "I doubt you're all that bad, honey. What are you . . . fourteen?"

I switched the channel with the remote. I stopped at a couple dancing in the rain and drinking 7Up. They made me want to cry. Was it fair for envy to be a sin? If you had everything, you could put envy out of your mind, but if you didn't, on top of everything else, you had to worry about wishing you had something!

I imagined Mr. Rappenhoe would have a quick reply to that, and it would sound nice, but not fit me at all.

"That's a cute ad, isn't it?" said Mrs. Zenor.

I looked at her, sitting on her couch, smiling. "Didn't you think God was wrong when He asked Abraham to sacrifice Isaac?" I asked.

She smoothed her hands over the lap of her puffy robe. Finally, with a little laugh, she said, "Well, He wasn't a father yet, Marie."

At first I liked her answer, but then I remembered: "He was God, Mrs. Zenor!"

"Yes."

"He was supposed to be *our* father, wasn't He?"

Mr. Zenor had been doing something in the basement. He came up the stairs just then, like on cue. "Girl talk?" he asked.

Mrs. Zenor patted my knee. "Let's discuss this in the morning, sweetie. Let's get some rest now," she said.

By ten-fifteen, except for the TV, the whole house was quiet. You would not have believed the quiet, like Krystal and I swam under the sea and all the others rode in a boat above. The weather lady said tomorrow would be the same as today, cold and clear. She acted as if she liked the prospect.

For cover, I left the TV on when I went in the kitchen. I put as many cans of formula as I could into a paper bag, along with half the Pampers, a jar of peanut butter, and a box of Triscuits.

I laid Krystal on the counter to change her. "You know you're going somewhere, don't you?" I said. She bounced her heels against me and laughed.

Have you ever noticed how babies cry and cry but don't understand *you* crying? Then somewhere along the line, maybe about the time they start *causing* pain, they get sad when you're sad.

I unbuttoned Krystal's little suit. She wiggled away from me, laughing. She had bruises from times when I didn't get between her and Dad and Anndean fast enough, and a burn scar on her thigh that nobody ever explained to my satisfaction, but she was, like Tommy, like all babies, perfect, perfection.

Maybe Anndean and Dad never felt sad about another person's pain in their life. Maybe they never felt bad enough themselves. Maybe they'd suffered too much and that was why they were the way they were, and God could look at the big picture and say, "A life's a short time, they'll rest with me in eternity." I didn't care. I didn't make them. I didn't have to ask their forgiveness for what I was about to do.

After I got Krystal suited up again and into her jacket, I checked the address for Mr. Rappenhoe's motel. It turned out it sat on the same stretch as the diner. Since I'd already stole the peanut butter and crackers, for which I guessed I'd be forgiven, I took the change on the windowsill, too. Three quarters and one dime. Enough for a cup of coffee at the truck stop, afterward.

Afterward.

At the thought—even though I held that wiggling little bundle of girl—my arms felt empty and strange, like when you stand in a doorway and press your hands against the frame, and then you step away, and up go your hands without your even willing.

In order to get myself through the Zenors' back door, I had to put the other children out of my head, and erase every thought of myself, too. Once I did that—even though it was bitter cold outside—I realized it was also clear and bright with fuzzy strands of stars high above.

The Amish houses I'd seen in the books at school were all big and white with clean yards. I imagined Chuck Rappenhoe's place like that.

I imagined myself stepping from such a house. Yes. I'm big and I'm solid and I pull on a cardigan as my husband, Chuck, pulls in the drive.

"Chuck," I call out, "welcome home!" Like my husband, I'm scarcely aware I radiate goodness, I'm just good, always work to be good, assume that's how it goes.

Chuck gets out of the car, grinning his old jack-o'-lantern grin. "Come here," he says. Excited, but almost whispering, like he doesn't want to wake somebody, "Come here!" So I laugh and come to the car, where he's pointing in the window at something I can't yet see, and he says, "Come see my little passenger!"

Then a big red car turns down the Zenors' street and in its bright headlights I become Marie again. Marie sticks out her thumb. The red car stops. The driver rolls down his window. "Hi, there," he says. He must not have a ceiling light but he strikes a match so I can see he's just a regular guy: ear muffs, freckles, an empty infant seat perched on his red vinyl upholstery, and somehow all of these things become the background for the burning message I now receive and the message is that by leaving behind my family, I do precisely what Jesus demanded of all true believers.

The man in the red car ducks his head down and forward, and he looks out at me and Krystal and he smiles like he knows something special is happening in our lives while he's just on his way to the store for diapers or beer or maybe a new clock radio. Do you see him? His earmuffs are rabbit fur. Do you see the way the red furnace of his car goes black and gray when his match dies? Answer yes or no, it hardly matters. What matters is the way I reply to his question, which is, "So, you need a ride?"

A trumpet blast. That's my reply. That's what matters, me as both trumpet and musician, servant and master, and the way my words— "I do"—just sail through the night, a bridal vow to the world.

Americans

LEFT HAND HOLDING open the pages of the strong, green journal lying on his desk, Oyekan wrote: "apple of my eye."

Mrs. Scotty Hillis had given Oyekan the journal not long after his arrival in the U.S. A sweet lady. Right to this very room she brought the green journal and three baked yams in a yellow dish. "I hope you'll be happy here," she had said.

Apple of my eye.

The blond-haired girl who sat next to Oyekan in Statistical Methods once told him he was "the apple of the teacher's eye." Oyekan did not know the expression, but felt it made easy sense, quite unlike Mr. Scotty Hillis's "If wishes were horses, beggars would ride," or, yesterday, the remark of Oyekan's friend Joe, at the barbershop: "Oyekan's got the Hillises eating out of his hand." *Eating out of his hand.* When Joe said this, the barber had made a smile, but still the words had not sounded nice.

Oyekan reached across his open journal to the chart hanging on the wall above his desk. "Border Changes in Nigeria." He slid a finger between the chart's colored transparencies. The top transparency—yellow—made his finger appear varnished; the second and third, dark as the back of a turtle.

Truly, Oyekan thought, his friend Joe was not himself lately. Truly, Joe was a good man. One day a month Joe did not eat so that money saved might be sent to poor peoples of the world. Soon he would go to Micronesia with the U.S. Peace Corps. Already, he volunteered at the medical center each Wednesday evening. And, too, Joe and his sweetheart, Peggy Dixon, had kindly taken Oyekan to lectures, films, parties, museums. This was America, all right! Peggy Dixon, herself a black girl, living in the U.S. just as comfy as a white boy like Joe! And no one even staring when they held hands.

"Peggy is the apple of my eye," wrote Oyekan. Then turned from his terrible, iridescent sentence—from where had it come?—and using his burnt sienna marker added quotation marks and, beneath the sentiment, the words "says Joe Hart."

Better. Yes. Soon Joe and Peggy would come to take Oyekan to the Internationals' Barbecue. Joe had hair of the marker's color, the color of the slim copper pipes running along the ceiling of Oyekan's basement bedroom in the fine, brick home of Mr. and Mrs. Scotty Hillis. Over Oyekan's head went the pipes, then straight into tidy holes in the paneled east wall, and beyond, to the shadowy, sweet bathroom where, since April, small mushrooms occasionally erupted at the toilet's base.

Our son this, our son that, Mr. and Mrs. Scotty Hillis had said the day Oyekan toured the big house and the son's bedroom that Oyekan was to use during his stay in the U.S. There were photographs of the son in the adjoining recreation room: golden Lee Hillis throws himself into a swimming pool whose surface appears dangerously white, a bath of mercury; handsome Lee on a motorcycle, still just long enough for the photographer to get the shot. During that little tour, Oyekan was still reeling from the long flight from Lagos, the fact of Minnesota. At least a week had passed before he understood the son to be not away, but dead, killed while engaged in an act which Mr. Scotty—face blotched red and white with grief—accorded the ominous, giddy name of "hang gliding."

A world away all of that seemed now, days when Oyekan did not yet know Mr. and Mrs. Scotty, or Joe and Peggy.

Oyekan laid down the burnt sienna marker, peered through his open door into the recreation room's dark. Only the blond shafts of the pool cues showed distinctly, but Oyekan knew the location of everything: the mini-tramp; the TV; the low table called, mysteriously, "the coffee table"; the photos. On the north wall was the photo that always struck Oyekan as most extraordinary, for it contained not only Lee Hillis but Oyekan's friend Joe, and Peggy Dixon, also. This made sense, of course. It was the Hillises who first introduced Oyekan to the couple. Many times he was told that Joe Hart had been best friend to Lee. Still. Visible proof. The dead son, Joe, Peggy. Whenever one wanted to examine:

All wore swimming suits and Lee Hillis appeared to laugh, perhaps at sunburned Joe, who, it seemed, had just kissed Peggy Dixon. Joe and beautiful Peggy smiled at each other with secret, impenetrable happiness. A smear of the white ointment on Joe's nose streaked Peggy's cheek—which made the picture not quite so nice, as it gave Peggy the look of a lost tribeswoman, and caused a heaviness in Oyekan's heart—

But stop! Soon his friends would arrive. He would tell them his good news.

At first, Oyekan had misunderstood Mrs. Scotty's tears at breakfast. Both he and Scotty Hillis had handed her their napkins, and, in her considerate way, Mrs. Scotty dabbed at her sweet, moon-round face with each in turn. Oyekan supposed that she cried at memory of the dead Lee. The old wife of Oyekan's father still cried at memory of one baby who died of measles some eighteen years before and, unlike Mrs. Scotty, the old wife had six children who lived.

Mrs. Scotty was too old for more children. Her hair was white as rice. Her hands lay motionless on the shiny tabletop, as if choked by their own thick, violet veins.

Oyekan looked across the breakfast table to Mr. Scotty. Was he glum, also? Mr. Scotty favored the word "pep." "I think a brisk walk would pep us up," he often said after dinner. Or, "Let's all go to the club for a swim! That'll get the sleep out of our eyes!" But this morning Mr. Scotty had sat quiet while Mrs. Scotty wept. Mr. Scotty chewed his bite of the English muffin. He wiped the crumbs off the breakfast nook table into one palm with the meaty side of the other.

Oyekan rose from his chair in the big blue and white kitchen. "What is it, please?" he pleaded. "May I help, then?"

"Oh, these are happy tears, sweetie," Mrs. Scotty said, "aren't they, Scotty?"

Mr. Scotty made the noises of a man digging heavy soil. "We'd like you to stay on with us, Oy," he said finally. "Like family. We thought Lee . . . the plant's growing every year."

The plant meant Hillis Carton, an impressively large and dusty concern that made wastepaper into boxes of cardboard.

Mr. Scotty continued: "You're a bright fellow, Oy. We know you've got opportunities back home, but we're awful fond of you, and there's a place in management for you right now, and more, you can bet on that."

Mrs. Scotty removed from her hair the single metal clip she inserted each night before bed. Absentmindedly, she worked its hinge: opened, closed, a hungry, long-beaked bird. "I can't imagine what it would be like around here without you now, Oy," she said.

"No." Mr. Scotty lifted his hands into the air. "No pressure, Edie. You don't have to answer right off. Oyekan. You sleep on it, see?"

As if he should need to "sleep on it"! Tears started to fill Oyekan's eyes. Did Mr. Scotty see this? Had he, too, felt as if he would begin to weep, or had shame at Oyekan's tears caused Mr. Scotty to carry his breakfast dishes over to the sink just then? His back to Oyekan and Mrs. Scotty, Mr. Scotty had said, "I know Peg and Joe would be happy if you stayed, Oy. I'd be willing to bet on that."

～

Yes! In a fit of high spirits, Oyekan now performed a series of pull-ups off the top of his bedroom door frame, dropped to the floor for sit-ups. Twenty-five, fifty, seventy-five.

"Hey, Oy, do twenty-five for me." So his friend Joe would tease if he were here. And then return to the reading of books of social injustices. And Peggy Dixon? Smiling, she would sit on the handsome red and gold bedspread, once Lee Hillis's, now Oyekan's.

One hundred! Happy in his brief exhaustion, Oyekan lay back on the carpet, fingered the bright loops of orange and brown and red. Everything about Minneapolis—its astonishing latitude and longitude, Mr. and Mrs. Scotty's generosity, the garage doors that went up and down at the touch of a button, clear lakes where handsome citizens canoed past homes gray and solid as fairy-tale castles—everything here affected him like the whiffs of Parsons' ammonia received when cleaning his bathroom: fascinating, purifying, liable to bring tears to his eyes. Bundles of energy thrilled the air! He stretched out a hand, laughing. He could grab a fistful of that energy, compress it—like the Minnesota snow, weightless flakes that, shaped into balls, became hard, might crack the windshield of an automobile.

A knot of poem forming in his belly pushed him upright:

> Your hair is dark and kinked as my own
> but, dressed with sweet oils,
> becomes a cloud of rainbows.

He would give this poem to Joe. To give to Peggy. But that made no sense! The excitement of the day had made him foolish; Joe's hair was neither dark nor kinked—

Gingerly, Oyekan lifted his fingertips to his new haircut. A terrible mistake. The day before he had accompanied Joe to the barbershop, where Joe—who always wore his hair in a battered left-hand parting—told the barber he wanted something "different." And when the man finished? Rusty curls rose out of the top of Joe's narrow, shaved head like froth on a glass of beer, so painfully awful that, as a comrade, Oyekan had felt the only thing he could do was to climb up in the chair and say, "Me, also."

He rose from the bedroom's bright carpet. Shyly, as if going to meet a stranger, he examined his reflection in the mirror that hung over the little bathroom sink.

How did he appear? When the barber had stopped his clipping, whisked away the silky apron, Oyekan had made a little joke: "And now I believe I am Frankenstein's monster!"

But the barber said, "Hey, Joseph, look at your handsome buddy, here. He looks like that Carl Lewis guy, doesn't he?"

Oyekan did not know any Carl Lewis.

"He was a celebrity," Joe had said. "Come on, I'll buy you a beer and you can sign my napkin."

Oyekan squinted at his reflection in the bathroom mirror. At home, they did not have a mirror, but a neighbor let them look in hers before town meetings and such. Americans were forever telling each other they resembled celebrities. Since arrival in the U.S., Oyekan had been told, also, he resembled the actor Harry Belafonte and a boxing star. At home, he resembled only his mother.

Suppose Peggy Dixon thought him a fool, an imitator of Joe's drastic gesture. Suppose, also, that on the way to the Internationals' Barbecue, in the confines of Joe's Datsun F10, he smelled of Mrs. Scotty's sauerkraut dish of last night.

Twice he brushed his teeth. The guide prepared by the Rotary Club stated that sometimes foreign students were "unfamiliar with accepted practices of hygiene." Oyekan and the other Internationals laughed about this at orientation, but it was not so funny the time a lady at the student union cafeteria backed away from Khabir with a show of disgust. "My friend does not want to be in your nose!" Oyekan told her. Scandalous! But she had not understood. Khabir had not understood. Oyekan had forgotten to use his English.

"Oy?"

Mrs. Scotty stood in the doorway, so cheerful in her bright skirt with black dogs following one another about the hem.

"I believe you are already to the barbecue, Mrs. Scotty?"

"On our way, sweetie. I just wanted to tell you"—she shifted a green lunch bucket decorated with flowers and birds and such from one hand to the other—"if you *do* decide to stay, Oy, I could write your mother for you. If you like . . ."

Oyekan's face grew hot. People would gather in the sunshine outside his mother's little house, chewing on cane, trying to hear the conversation inside, between his mother and brother. Biki, too, and at her side the old gray and yellow dog that followed her always, to the fields and the pump and the market. Biki might understand; before his departure she teased that he would be like Daniel Ojay, who went to USC to study chemical engineering and never returned, broke his betrothal. Oyekan's mother, however, would not understand. His mother would pull on the clothes and hands of Oyekan's brother. She would plead: "How can this be? Is he in trouble there? Is he in jail? Is he sick?"

"I thank you, Mrs. Scotty," said Oyekan. "But I would have to write—"

"Of course. Of course, you would, dear." She lowered her head after that, as if afraid; the exact gesture of his mother when she learned of the scholarship to the U.S.

"Mrs. Scotty . . . ," Oyekan began, but, outside, Mr. Scotty began to honk the horn of his auto impatiently, and Mrs. Scotty hurried toward the door.

"I know you'll make the right decision," she said. "I just know it."

∼

The thick tires of Mr. and Mrs. Scotty's auto rolled past his bedroom window, and for one moment his room became dark, but then the light returned.

Suppose Peggy Dixon called and said that Joe did not wish to go to the barbecue today, but that she and Oyekan might go anyway?

Oyekan wanted to see Joe, of course, but he had such news today and lately, Joe appeared most often deep in thought, and, then, to draw him forth, Peggy Dixon would begin telling noisy tales; after Oyekan's Honors' presentation, it had been the story of a drunken cousin, drowned in an attempt to retrieve a bottle of whiskey from a flooded building called a "fallout shelter."

Ho, ho, ho, this made Joe and Peggy laugh and laugh.

Oyekan was sorry, but he did not see the humor.

That same night, at Peggy's apartment, he and Peggy and Joe had watched an old television program in which a man received a wound and discovered himself to be a robot. As if they saw themselves in the robot man who did not know himself to be a robot, Peggy and Joe cried. They cried! They laughed! Sometimes Oyekan did not understand Peggy and Joe at all. Oyekan was no robot! His blood ran hot in him, thank you very much! Joe was a good friend, a good man, but if Oyekan were Joe, he would not act so silly before Peggy Dixon. He would not rush off to Micronesia, leaving her to be sought after by other males, no way!

Maybe Joe did not like Peggy so well after all. In Joe's place, Oyekan would write Peggy poems and take her interesting places—perhaps on a motorcycle like Lee Hillis's, certainly not in a rusty Datsun F10 with gravel and squashed fast food containers in the back. He would show good posture and never fall down on the floor laughing during the *Saturday Night Live* television show, an act Oyekan witnessed after Joe and Peggy believed him gone, after the robot television show.

He had been wrong to watch. His dear friends. They had not even wanted him to leave. All the way to the door, Peggy teased, "Won't you stay on just a bit, Oyekan, now we're having such fun?" Peggy Dixon's eyes were flecked with green. She spoke with the accent of the American South, her voice soft and deep as pillows. Down the dark little hall she called to Joe, "Joseph, come on out here and instill a little guilt in this friend of yours, so he won't go breaking up our party." Peggy had held in her fingers the cloth of Oyekan's jacket so that his hand might not fit through the sleeve. The two of them had stood there, together, watching for Joe to appear at the end of the hall, but Joe had never come and, eventually, Peggy let go of the sleeve. She looked beyond Oyekan, out the apartment door, her gay voice suddenly sad. "You didn't like me telling that story about Roy drowning in the fallout shelter, did you?"

"You are a good storyteller, Peggy," Oyekan said, "but I think your stories have the problem that they lie. They pretend to ask only for laughter. This is not right. A story may lie and lie, but all its lies must tell the truth in the end."

"Whoa!" Joe stood at the end of the hall, his feet clad only in athletic stockings. "It was so quiet out here I figured you'd gone, Oy!"

"I'm trying to get him to stay, Joe," said Peggy. She turned back to Oyekan, smiling. "Come on, now, we'll make you a fine big bowl of popcorn. Popcorn with butter on it!"

But Oyekan left. That he might stand in the open, second-story stairwell of the apartment building across the way and, leaning over the balustrade in a manner that caused passersby to stare, observe whether or not Peggy and Joe behaved differently in his absence.

They watched television, made popcorn.

Then a neighbor had threatened to call police officers if Oyekan did not move along, and so he had missed whatever came next.

Where were they now, Peggy and Joe? Oyekan looked at his digital watch: 1:23 P.M. The clock radio beside his bed read 1:31. They might be late, or not yet due.

The previous fall, when Joe and Peggy came to Mr. and Mrs. Scotty's for dinner—the night Oyekan met the younger couple—why, no sooner had he and Mrs. Scotty stepped into the dining room to insert the clever extra piece in Mrs. Scotty's shiny table than Joe and Peggy had begun to kiss! And not in a polite way, but with hands moving, mouths open!

Would they be doing this now?

To still himself, Oyekan noted the previous day's high and low temperatures in his journal. The coldest day of the year since Oyekan's arrival had been January twenty-third. He used to imagine reading from the journal to his family. Everyone would laugh at such cold, his stories of foolish American university girls, the loss of his new penny loafer shoe in the first snow. Back then, the journal drew him on, it extracted the gifts he wanted to share. Now, he felt the others would understand nothing of his recent entries; and the early entries no longer amused him, showed only what a bumpkin he had been.

The ringing of telephones still made Oyekan jump. Even when one knew one was to receive a call, even if one waited with the hand holding the phone, the ringing happened behind one's back, nasty as Oyekan's auntie's monkey throwing its messes. Oyekan put his fingers in his ears as he walked into the recreation room. He had lived twenty-two years without a telephone and never felt the lack. This would be a rule in his U.S. home: No telephone!

"Are you ready?"

"Peggy," said Oyekan. The high school graduation photo of Lee Hillis sat on the stereo. It seemed that daring, golden boy offered advice. Oyekan could say, "I have a surprise for you and Joe!" But, in fact, he said only, "I am thinking perhaps I will study this afternoon, Peggy."

"Oh, Oy!" Peggy cried. "Mr. and Mrs. Hillis helped plan this! Besides, I personally know the picnic features ham, potato salad *slathered* with mayonnaise, and watermelon from Texas! Chocolate brownies with chocolate icing! Food our kidnapped ancestors ate to ease their aching hearts!"

Kidnapped ancestors. As if both descended from slaves.

Joe Hart took the phone from Peggy. "As you can see, Oy, she's wired," he said.

"Wired." Which meant, Oyekan knew, excited.

~

"My, my!" Peggy called as he walked briskly around the car and slid into the backseat. Embarrassed, tantalized by the possibility that she truly did believe his haircut handsome, he said, sternly, "You do not wear your seat belt. Either of you."

Peggy laughed. Her lips bore the hot red color of the flowers planted by Mrs. Scotty that very morning. *Geraniums.* Her hair was sleek today, bound into a tiny, most elegant knot at the base of the neck; and, to his surprise, she wore a long skirt similar to that worn by women of his own region. She pulled at the seat belt. "I do believe I'm getting fat as a hippo!" she cried.

"No, no," Oyekan began; but there were Joe's eyes in the rearview mirror, watching, and they flickered away as if Joe did not mean for Oyekan to see.

Too late! Oh, terrible, terrible. Joe now knew what lay so deep in Oyekan's heart, and so did Oyekan.

Heart jumping, mouth dry, Oyekan hurried on: "Now, I first became a stick in the U.S. You may see this in photos from the Thanksgiving Day. My skin became gray like ash, my clothes no longer fitted!" He forced himself to look, once again, into the mirror, and to grin. "Now, however, I am a slick dog, man! I eat Mr. Scotty's chocolate chocolate chip ice cream each dinner. My belt is size thirty-four inches. This morning, Mrs. Scotty tells me I cannot wear my old shirts anymore. I am not decent!"

Peggy Dixon smiled at Oyekan over her shoulder. "This one boyfriend to my mama, now he *loved* ice cream. That was Floyd Barstow. Y'all remember Floyd, the one she was carousing with the time she met up with Daddy and *his* honey on that painfully narrow bridge—"

Joe interrupted with a laugh, "And Floyd's car and your dad's car got wedged together—"

Peggy Dixon clapped her hand over her mouth.

"Go on," said Joe.

She shook her head. "No. I don't want to tell that. Oy, you tell us something sane and good. Tell us . . . what you hear from home. Tell us news of your Biki."

Oyekan smiled, but pretended to take the words of Peggy Dixon as outcry, in no way a genuine request. He was sick at heart, and this— American politeness! They thought betrothal crazy, but that their politeness required they act as if Biki were his heart's desire, that he had chosen her for the foolish reasons they chose each other! In this way, they were bad as children—worse! Like monkeys trained to drink tea from a cup.

Joe slowed the car. "We want ten nineteen. Ten twenty-seven. And . . . this must be it."

Oyekan peered up a long driveway to a large and angular home. Tending the barbecue grills on the wooden porches that wrapped the house were Mrs. Scotty, and Professor McCall, too, her lower half encased in a pair of vast and surprising pink pants.

The car came to a crackling stop on the gravel drive. Miserable, ashamed—what right did he have to be angry with Joe?—Oyekan tried to make a little laughter for his friends: "I am the apple of Professor McCall's eye."

Peggy Dixon smiled as she bent down for the big covered bowl at her feet. "Is Oyekan practicing his ironing?" she asked. An old joke. All three laughed as they climbed from the car. "Irony is commonplace in modern literature," the teacher of American novels had told Oyekan's class; Oyekan had misheard.

Peggy Dixon set her bowl on the roof of the car. Sunshine shot through its translucent contents. That would be her gelatin dessert filled with pears and the delicious fluffy bits called marshmallows.

"I'm tired of irony," Peggy Dixon drawled. "I do believe modern literature could use more ironing."

"Hey." Joe laid his hand on Oyekan's arm. Forgiveness? Oyekan glanced toward Peggy Dixon, busy rolling up her window.

"Joe," Oyekan began in a quiet rush, "if you believe I have over-stepped—"

"This is Lee's shirt, isn't it?"

Oyekan looked down in confusion at the shirt front. "Yes. You see, Joe, Mrs. Scotty . . ."

Joe shrugged. "Forget it, man. I just wondered." He winked. "It looks good on you."

"So be it, Joe," said Oyekan, though he did not believe the wink of his friend sincere. "So be it. Do you wish me to carry your dish, Peggy?"

Joe laughed, his head turned toward Peggy Dixon, now busy with the hiding of her purse beneath the front seat. "Peggy's a big girl, Oy," he said. "Hell, she *used* to pick me up and carry me into the bedroom whenever the urge hit her."

"Joe!" Peggy rose from the car with a movement too quick, and bumped her head on the roof; but Joe did not stop to offer apologies. Joe crossed the lawn, through girls in blue jeans, and men in turbans, dashikis, Muslim women in their headdresses of gray and black wool. Under high pine trees, a group of Indian students played volleyball. "Hey!" called a plump girl in a purple sari as Joe passed through their game, but play continued uninterrupted, a score was made.

"Oh," Peggy moaned. Oyekan did not wish to look at her. The image of Joe in her arms—his heart shook his chest, it was swollen, inflamed. He did not know whether he wished to weep on the shoulder of Joe or smash his fists into his friend's face.

"Look at this," he said angrily and indicated with a jerk of his head a girl of Mexico he had met on another such occasion. Big yellow streaks in her dark hair that made her look like a tiger. A chubby girl who, it seemed to him now, always had behaved as if she thought herself better than the other internationals because her country sat next to the U.S. Today she wore a leopard print bikini and stood beside the diving board, shivering, jiggling her knees and shoulders. "Such a fool, to come in such clothes," he said.

Peggy shook her head, then whispered, "She probably got her sights set on some fellow at this picnic, Oy, and she's putting all her merchandise on the counter. Who's she got to love her here, poor thing, all her folks back home?" Peggy sighed. "Now where do you suppose a body's to put a dish? I do hate the first minutes at big parties. Someday, somebody—I *know* it—is going to mistake me for help and send me out to wash up glasses!"

Oyekan softened at this admission. She was so pretty, so kind, and here was her forehead all wrinkled with worry. "Not at this party, Peggy, though here we maybe are all potential dishwasher material!" He laughed. "Do you know, such a thing did happen at Mr. and Mrs. Scotty's golfing club? In the coat room, a member asks if I might bring his car!"

"No!"

He held up a finger, tapped the air. "I only report this to show it happened, and still I live." He smiled. "Undiminished, yes?"

"Undiminished," said Peggy. "You . . ." She dragged her long fingernails along the back of one of her hands. Faint trails of roughed skin remained when she finished, and she looked up from them as if surprised, and embarrassed, too. "You . . . do you think she's pretty, Oy, the Mexican girl?" she asked, and then, before he could answer, "Do I ever remind you of anybody from home?"

The question lodged in his chest, hot as the heart shown by Jesus Christ in the room Gloria Dei Church loaned for practice of English conversation. Oyekan looked at the plump Mexican girl—so strangely sexual and sexless in her silly clothing, one leg extended before herself, as if she imagined herself in a magazine of American fashion.

Peggy Dixon brought her face close. She stood, perhaps, thirty centimeters taller than his betrothed, her eyes of green flecks almost on a level with his own. She resembled no one, anywhere.

But one learned to deal with such terrible questions in America, and, with the sleeves of Lee Hillis's old shirt rolled above his biceps, his feet springy on their cushion of socks and running shoes, Oyekan felt . . . almost American. He found an American grin. He asked Peggy Dixon, "When?"

Peggy Dixon covered her mouth with her fingertips. "Don't you mean 'who'?"

Still grinning, Oyekan shook his head, no. But this made Peggy Dixon look away, her eyes suddenly sad. "There's Mr. Scotty," she murmured. She waved at Scotty Hillis, down on the lawn, a set of colored wooden mallets and balls in his hand. "You're getting burned, y'all!" she called. "Better get that head covered!"

Mr. Scotty nodded and smiled. To Oyekan's relief, Peggy looked back at him, laughing.

"Mr. Scotty enjoys a small consequence," he said.

"He's a sweetheart," said Peggy.

"He's a bear!" Mrs. Scotty, coming up from behind, put an arm around each. "And don't you two make a handsome couple!" She flushed, widened her eyes, as if she, too, were startled by her words. "With Oyekan's haircut, I mean! I can't quite get used to it! How'd Joe's turn out, Peggy? I haven't seen him yet."

Peggy Dixon smiled at Oyekan as if she had not even heard the embarrassing words of Mrs. Scotty! "Well, Joe wanted something different," she said with a laugh, "and different he got. I don't doubt but the boy'll be a big hit in Truk, or wherever they send him off to!"

Mrs. Scotty laughed at this, also, her face tilted up to the sunshine. "So!" She rubbed her hand briskly up and down Oyekan's arm. "Scotty says I'm not to pester you, Oy, but I'll bet Peggy and Joe agree you should stay!"

"Oy?" Peggy Dixon leaned forward and squeezed his hand.

Perhaps she did indeed remind him of someone from home, and he had not recognized this until she put on the traditional skirt? But no, it was the smile he recognized, so sleepy, so secret. And not from home at all: the smile offered Joe in the photograph in the recreation room. The smile after the kiss. For him now, Oyekan.

"Mr. and Mrs. Scotty are most kind," Oyekan said, his voice no more than a whisper.

Down on the lawn, Joe held a handful of the wire hoops that Mr. Scotty bent to press into the grass. Mrs. Scotty was saying to Peggy Dixon, "I guess I don't have to tell you Oy's like family," while Mr. Scotty was talking to Joe. Mr. Scotty lifted his red face to point in the direction of Oyekan. Mr. Scotty waved and smiled, and Joe looked up also, his face white as tooth, bone.

Perhaps Joe meant to smile, but could not. Oyekan himself could not smile. Teeth pressed together, he looked at Peggy, at Mrs. Scotty—both of them waiting to be happy, already weary with waiting, their smiles veiled with the wait.

"Oy?" said Peggy Dixon.

He backed into the line of people traveling past the many bowls of food, gathering baked beans and brownies and salads. "Excuse me," he said. "Excuse me, please."

~

The door to the big house stood closed. On the small pane of glass that allowed those inside to look out at callers was a note that read, "Picnickers: Please use bathhouse loo!"

Oyekan pushed open the door. He stepped inside. Darkness and the chemical cold of conditioned air filled the house, a shock after the bright afternoon. Quickly, he passed through many rooms of beige carpet, brick, wood. He meant to convey acquaintance with the house should anyone see him, but to his surprise all of the rooms stood empty, quiet, curtained against the sun.

In the end, he sat down in the single chair of a small room he took to be a kind of study, walls lined with books and, too, dolls from foreign countries: an Asian doll with a load of twigs on his back; a Spanish dancer with wide skirts of orange and red and pink; a Scotsman playing the bagpipes. Oyekan fitted his back to the chair. He took deep breaths to calm himself. In, out. Out. The sound of the picnickers reached him as a kind of rustle, a small and uniform wave of gaiety that washed against the outer walls of the big house.

He sat in the chair for a very long time, long after he had grown used to the dark and come to see that the shadow caught in the room's pale curtains was not a fold of the curtain's cloth, but the Mexican girl from the swimming pool, and that she was in hiding, too.

Beautiful Land

THOUGH SHE HAD hardly known it back in 1951, Gwen Vander Schaaf had been in love with Randall Decker. She had known, of course, that when she sat behind Randall in homeroom, she'd studied the way his close-cropped hair made an opalescent sheen across his perfect skull. And that when Randall leaned far, far back to look at her, and laid his head right upon her desktop, she often found a way to touch him—sometimes with the provocative pink nipple of a pencil eraser. Still, along with all the chores Randall Decker had had to perform on his father's farm, he'd had to bear himself up under the gray burden of Decker family life, and so the socks that hung around Randall's ankles had made Gwen think of the just-loosened ropes of hangmen, and there were his dazzling blue eyes—one or the other always in some state of blackening. Too, a great oozing patch of scab often marred that perfect skull of Randall's. And all of this together meant that the fact of loving Randall never knocked loudly enough at the gates to the world Gwen Vander Schaaf proposed for herself in 1951.

So maybe it wasn't love anyway? Maybe not?

Gwen had dated Thom Muller back in 1951. Twelve years ago now.

When she and Thom Muller had danced together in the Morrow gymnasium on Friday nights, Gwen made her breasts high and tight, but did not allow Thom Muller to press his thigh against her own, and thus she garnered a reputation as that most desirable of girls—one both passionate and pure—though, in fact, she knew herself to be neither with regard to Thom Muller, and could never understand all the work she and the other girls did to secure places in the hearts of a town they dreamt only of escaping.

The whole of high school, Randall Decker had gone to just one dance: senior prom. Without a date. All that night, Gwen felt as if something magical were about to happen, Randall would put down the bottle of Coke he nursed over by the door, push himself off the gymnasium wall, and, with one of his long, fine fingers, tap on Thom's shoulder. But the prom drew to a close. Thom guided Gwen toward the door. There stood Randall, blowing hollow notes across the top of his empty bottle. As if she were gorgeously amused, did not see Randall at all, Gwen threw back her head in laughter. Randall reached out to her, then drew his finger down her bare arm and whispered, "You girl," words that dropped over Gwen like a silver net, cold and beautiful and impossible to escape.

"What'd he say?" Thom wanted to know.

"He said my hair looked pretty."

And Thom said, "It looks the same as always."

In 1951, Gwen wore her hair in a pageboy, rolled each night around a fresh sanitary napkin pad: an extravagance, and an outrage against decency, which her Dutch Reformed father did not allow a place at the breakfast table.

Suppose she had turned back to Randall that night—the way she wanted—and she had ended up married to him? Suppose even *one* of the reunions she imagined over the years had actually come true? Would she have brought Randall luck and happiness?

Gwen thought of all this now, looking out the wavy glass of the teachers' lounge window, as Randall's little daughter, Lily, climbed down from the school bus and walked toward the elementary wing of

Morrow Consolidated. Last off the bus. Small for a fourth grader. Perfect braids, one hung over the right shoulder, one hung over the left. Proceeded precisely down the middle of the walk. Careful to avoid thawed muck. Looking back as the bus pulled away as if perhaps someone called her name.

No one there. Just the houses and then the hills.

~

When the small students of Morrow Consolidated drew horizons upon sheets of manila, those horizons ran straight from one border to the other, broken only by a piece or two of subject matter: a cozy house curling smoke into the sky, a horse, a dog barking at a ferocious, oversize tulip. The true horizon of Morrow, however, was hump after hill, each rise swollen, sliding behind the other like racks of bread, waves, the regular, repetitious beauty of delirium.

Now that spring was coming, the more ambitious fields—plowed the fall before—lay black and ready against the hills' even sedge. In the dimples of the hills, the last tucks of snow appeared pure white, though at close range they were honeycombed, speckled with dirt.

From Morrow's hills, the town's leafless but plentiful branches of oaks and lindens and maples moved in the wind, seemed almost a swarm above the houses; white, most of them, with a single car garage set off to the back of the lot. The wet gravel streets were the color of coarse mustard and—pulling onto the stretch of highway that slowed for Morrow—local cars and school buses and trucks drew a wash of gravel onto the highway's asphalt, left behind twin fans of ochre at every intersection.

The highway ran by the school yard. There, children gathered at their appointed doors to enter for the day. The oldest students—girls with hair ratted and sprayed in imitation of what they saw on trips to Sioux City; boys dreaming of joining the Navy in May—moved into the senior wing in orderly fashion. They ignored the photographs that hung in the halls: their grandparents, young themselves in those days, standing on the steps of the original schoolhouse, torn down in 1919 and replaced by the flat-roofed building that now housed Elementary.

One shrewd teacher in that pre-Depression community had suggested that the school install a peaked roof, and situate its hallways along the north side of the building; this, she contended, would prevent the school's looking like a factory, save electricity, and buffer the classrooms against winter winds. Other parties, however, favored the symmetry of industrialization. They opted for a flat roof and the dark, central halls through which Elementary's children currently stumbled:

Elementary's janitor, Mr. Menecke, had forgotten to turn on the fluorescents before going up on the roof to hack at the ice that accumulated there every winter and—melting—seeped down, dark as tea, into the sickroom below.

On the roof, Mr. Menecke swore vilely. Mr. Menecke threw broken ice over the eaves, sometimes without even looking to see if a child might pass below. Back then, people did not count on bad luck and disaster the way they would learn to do in the years to come. Mr. Menecke regularly set the schoolgirls in his lap and kissed them in a manner that many of them did not like, but did not know how to protest. Elementary was full of asbestos and a fire trap besides. In the dark hall, the children moved like potatoes spilled from a bag. They bumped against one another's legs and arms. They galloped and scuffled—

～

"You ignoramus!" So cried Lily Decker to a boy with a broad, flat face, and she pointed at the shoe she had, until then, managed to keep clean by great efforts—crisscrossing the muddy lane that led from her grandparents' farmhouse to the main road, avoiding other children on the bus.

"Biggy wow, Lily," the boy called over his shoulder, "a little mud!"

"Clod! Piker!" These were names Lily's grandfather called her father. Ignoramus. Lazy lout. Plus things you should not repeat even in your head. Like last summer, when Lily and her mother and father had first moved from Massachusetts onto her grandfather's farm. Lily had been given a dish towel to shoo flies from the peaches not yet put into jars. Not much of a job, which was why she was looking out the window at her grandma's bean plants at just the moment her father ran across the burnt yard and crashed into the dark kitchen from the bright outdoors. Close on his heels came Lily's grandfather, who paused in the doorway to scream a terrible name, then pitched an entire crate of peaches at Lily's father's back.

What terrible thing had her father done that day? Bent three tines of something her grandfather called a "disc." And what had he done after her grandfather went back outside? Sat in one of the kitchen chairs and wept.

Now Lily crouched, rubbed at her smeared shoe with the piece of tissue her mother always tucked in her pocket before school.

"That's quite a getup, Lily. Birthday party today?"

Miss Vander Schaaf. Elementary's secretary. Lily did not like Miss Vander Schaaf, who wore short-sleeved sweaters that showed too much of her chubby arms, and always smiled as if they shared a secret.

"My dad's coming to take me today."

"Ah."

Lily did not watch the woman back into the lounge. Everyone in Morrow turned pink and red when Lily mentioned her father's name, as if she should pretend he did not even exist. She tugged on the tips of her gloves to remove them, little tugs that did not make the gloves end up inside out. Her mother had taught her how to do this. Almost everyone said her mother resembled the beautiful actress Loretta Young. How Lily's father could have left such a kind and pretty woman was a grave mystery.

Red gloves with green vines and white flowers with a yellow French knot in the middle. Lily's grandparents did not believe in celebrating Christmas, but Lily's mother had given her the gloves, anyway. The right one had a pocket on its back. The pocket held a lucky penny and a chip of blue and white porcelain. Over breakfast on

Christmas morning, Lily's mother had explained that the penny and chip were lucky pieces because she had turned them up in the garden the day she learned she was pregnant with Lily. The story had made Lily's grandparents lift their full cheeks, stare at each other, chew hard on the fried potatoes and eggs.

~

The chat with Lily Decker left Gwen feeling breathless, the way she had felt after her last trip to the city when, stopped at a red light, forgetting that red lights were not the same as stop signs, she pulled into the intersection and was almost crushed between cars speeding at her from the left and the right.

So. She rapped together a stack of multiple choice tests for Third. "So," she said to the lounge's only other inhabitant, Dale Mulford, "so, that Decker's coming by today for his girl."

"Mm." Dale Mulford was the principal, a slender man with a cockade of brown hair atop his head. He frowned to indicate preoccupation with the task at hand: cutting a wedge of peppermint cake from a pan on the table. He did not like gossip, but he knew the basic Decker story. The man had moved his wife and child from Massachusetts to his parents' farm, then abandoned them for some Sioux City woman. The citizenry of Morrow couldn't get enough of the Decker story and, as if to oblige, over Christmas, the girlfriend had stabbed Decker in the back. How many times? Some said three, some four, no one said two, which Dale Mulford eventually learned was the correct answer.

Dale Mulford came from Sioux City, and held the firm opinion that no one in Morrow ever accepted a thing at face value. Everyone in Morrow went about crabbed with guilt and discomfort and a ridiculous sense of the superiority this conferred, like a woman proud she managed to cram her foot into a shoe several sizes too small.

"So, Gwen, did you try this lovely cake Floria brought?"

"At eight in the morning?" Gwen gave him the locals' wide-eyed look of incredulity, swallowed it with some show, as if she believed such dramatics constituted good manners.

"So." In as pleasant a voice as he could muster, Dale asked, "So where'd Decker's wife come from, anyway?"

"Oh, who knows!" said Gwen, though the answer was Freiburg, a city she had looked up in the atlas and held on the map of her heart ever after. What anguish she had felt the night Thom Muller came by to take her dancing, and glibly announced, "I guess Randall Decker got engaged to some girl he met stationed over there"!

That night, Gwen had wrenched Thom Muller's ring from her finger and thrown it on the dance floor. The dance came to a stop as Rhonda Hansen set her foot down on the big ring and stumbled forward into a neighboring couple, who had turned to watch Thom Muller stalk from the gymnasium. Gwen prayed that word of the spectacle would reach Randall at his base in Germany. Randall would come. Randall and Gwen would escape, take new names in a new land.

~

Her fingers on the drinking fountain handle, Lily looked up at the photo of the Class of 1951. When her father arrived at eleven, she would say, nonchalantly, "I guess I forgot my bag on the breezeway. I guess we'll have to stop by the farm."

The boys in the Class of 1951 looked *old*, didn't they, as if being of another era aged them in their frames? They seemed men, despite the silly knobs of hair so many of them wore on top of their heads. A classmate of Lily's had one of those old-fashioned oily knobs and, once, after he made a smart remark about her dad, she said, "What's with your hair, Glen? You let your mom use it to wipe out the bacon pan?"

Could she really have said something so awful? She really could have.

In his photo, Lily's father looked handsome, but also like someone from whom you shouldn't take a ride. He still looked like that, she supposed, only thinner. Since the stabbing, the bones of his cheeks seemed chipped from stone, like the flaked arrowheads he'd collected on the farm as a boy.

Last month, he had visited Lily for the first time since the stabbing. He wore a new orange sweater decorated with diamonds of brown and gray vinyl. In order to avoid meeting him when he came by, Lily's grandparents and mother had driven the family Ford up the road and parked under a clump of cottonwoods. Lily's Aunt Cara had stayed at the house with Lily. Cara cried in the kitchen. Lily sat quietly in the front room. Her father took her hand in his own. "I want you to know," he said, "I'd never let anyone hurt you."

An odd thing to say. He, after all, was the one who'd been hurt. Still, Lily had to let him say what he wanted to say, and then nod, as if she believed him.

The newspaper had run a photograph of his girlfriend, Mrs. Kramer. WOMAN STABS LOVER. A lumpy, weary woman—*old*—who seemed to be staring at a pop bottle someone had set on top of the waiting squad car.

After the stabbing, once Lily knew her father would live, Lily had believed the worst was over, he'd come home. Well, he hadn't. And, last night, on the telephone, he'd talked on and on about Mrs. Kramer. He wanted Lily to meet her. "You mustn't hate her, Lily," he said. "She's been in the hospital ever since, and I . . . provoked her, you see."

Lily had felt ashamed. And in pain, too. His words were a bullet that contained the secret of him, a bullet lodged in her heart in such a way that only dangerous surgery could remove it, present it for understanding.

"Hey, Lily."

The girl turned. Beside her stood Christine De Vries. "That's my Uncle Leland in the picture next to your dad. They were friends in high school."

Lily bent to drink from the fountain. The day she and the others had come back from the disastrous Christmas vacation, Lily had spied the children studying the photograph of the Class of 1951. Christine

De Vries stood among them, smiling, talking, just the way she talked to Lily when Mrs. De Buhr had "buddied" them for the field trip to Sioux Bee Honey.

Lily lifted her mouth from the fountain, wiped her hand across her wet mouth. "My father hated this school," she said as she hurried around Christine. One lie, and then another: "He couldn't stand this dinky town."

≈

Morrow Consolidated had a problem for which no solution had been devised: Elementary's classrooms groaned with the pressure of all those well-fed, postwar babies. Ancient desks with inkwells in their upper-right-hand corners had been retrieved from the hay loft over the bus barn. Lily had to pick her way through the narrow aisles in order to give Mrs. De Buhr the note from her mother. Mrs. De Buhr— formerly an excellent teacher, now beleaguered—snapped, "You'll excuse yourself *quietly!*"

While Lily made her way to her desk, Mrs. De Buhr turned on the classroom TV and Clark Hinshaw, the TV instructor of *Your Iowa,* was soon opening the tailgate of his station wagon and taking out his easel. Clark Hinshaw wore a coat and hat, but no muffler or gloves. Behind him, the trees appeared bare as the trees in Morrow. Christine De Vries had once told Lily that Clark Hinshaw worked in a TV studio and what you saw behind him was just a photograph. Unlike Christine, Lily hadn't been disappointed, but thrilled at the lengths to which the program went to provide the audience with the illusion that Clark Hinshaw stood at the various Iowa sites.

"Of course, you students know Indians once inhabited Iowa," said Clark Hinshaw. "Think of Sioux City, named after the Sioux." Mrs. De Buhr's students grinned at one another. A few hollered, "Yea! Sioux City!"

"Maquoketa," said Mr. Hinshaw. "Cherokee. The very name of our state comes from the Indians. Do you know the meaning of Iowa, girls and boys?"

Mrs. De Buhr, at work at her desk, lifted her head and looked out at the class. Dutifully, the students responded, "Beautiful Land!"

"Beautiful Land," said Clark Hinshaw. With a piece of charcoal, he drew a large question mark on his easel pad. "Today we're going to visit the Effigy Mounds and explore the questions surrounding them. Most important: Were these very sophisticated mounds, with their evidence of advanced culture, built by some lost mysterious tribe? Or"—Clark Hinshaw turned his pad upside down, used the question mark's curve as the foundation for the enormous nose of a frowning Indian—"or could the mounds have been built by Iowa's Indians themselves?"

According to Clark Hinshaw, the Mound Builders showed great sophistication: buried their dead with beads, pipes, tools, and ceramic vessels. Seashells among the artifacts suggested the tribe participated in trade. They experimented with corn, squash, sunflowers, and beans—

Lily looked out the window to the highway beyond. Empty. She had seen Indians once, just after she and her mother and father moved to Iowa. The family had gone to Sioux City to buy Randall coveralls. They were parking the car when they saw a man in the street, his pants not pulled up properly. The woman who was his companion cried while the man crawled in the road. "Drunk," said Lily's father, then put money into the parking meter and started off down the sidewalk. Lily's mother stopped, though, and helped the woman guide the man onto the grass. She gave the woman the money meant for the coveralls. There was a small boy, too. Somehow the woman had attached his snow pants to a lilac bush so he wouldn't run after her into the street.

Clark Hinshaw seemed to believe that the Indians of Iowa *had* been the Mound Builders. Lily didn't want to believe it, but she supposed it was true. "Thousands of mounds!" said Clark Hinshaw. "And to have built just *one* would have required one thousand men working for one hundred years!"

One thousand men. One hundred years. And where did they go?

What happened to their world? When white settlers reached Iowa,
Clark Hinshaw said, the Indians who remained appeared little more
than savages.

~

Out on the highway, a tractor-trailer rig made a clownish noise as it
slowed for the Morrow patrol car. Mayflower, read the truck. A sil-
houette of a ship in yellow and green.

Lily owned a book about a trucker. In the clearest of watercolor
washes—greens and blues and Easter egg yellows—the book's trucker
takes his small son and daughter on a haul. The three drink cold milk
from a thermos and eat bologna sandwiches. The boy and girl take
turns napping in the sleeper while the responsible dad guides them
through the wonder of a night filled with all of the stars the children
have never before been up late enough to see. All in all, the book suggested the children's world contained more good things than they'd
ever realized, and that more lay ahead.

Lily remembered little of her father's trucking except the dank,
clammy way he smelled when he came home, and how he spent his
free days in the cellar, smoking cigarettes. There was an accident with
his rig. Then another. Over supper, one evening, he told Lily's mother,
"I can't keep the truck on the road anymore." Almost like a complaint.
As if he believed Lily's mother ought to solve the problem; it was no
more serious than a tear in his pants, or a broken zipper.

While they talked, Lily went down into the cellar. She had never
spent time there—a dark, damp place—and it seemed to her she
needed to be someplace unfamiliar, maybe she would find something
that helped. Near the base of the cellar stairs lay a salamander: black,
its back covered with stars like the stars in the story about the truck
ride, but when she reached out to touch the salamander, it skittered
under the stairs.

Her father had robbed them, hadn't he? Taken away their happiness before she could even learn what it might be.

~

At five to eleven she put on her coat and gloves and went to stand by Elementary's front entrance. Between glances out the door, she studied the mosaic on the wall beside her. It was made of nothing but corn. Indian corn, field corn, popcorn fitted together to form warped buffalos and barns and fractured tractors. Something meant to resemble the state's wild rose had been done up out of popcorn enameled with a pink polish meant for fingernails. "Iowa," read the mosaic's legend. "Beautiful Land."

At 11:10, Lily unsnapped the pocket on her glove, taking out the porcelain chip. Her mother had told Lily that if she were to see an entire plate of the porcelain pattern—Blue Willow—she would see the legend of two lovers taking flight over a bridge from the cruel father who wished to prevent their marriage. In the legend, the gods took pity on the lovers and turned them into doves.

Lily realized that her mother imagined the story as some convoluted version of her own tale, and so she never shared what she discovered at the library:

In China, hundreds and hundreds of years ago, revolutionaries sent round the Blue Willow plates to remind their followers of their aim to overthrow the government. The three figures on the bridge represented Past, Present, and Future; the doves, the souls of those already slain in battle.

Lily did not like it that the plates said one thing to mean another, but she understood. The plates had a secret, something that could not safely be said aloud.

At 11:20, the other children began to file past, on their way to lunch.

"Where's your dad?" Christine De Vries asked.

"He got held up," said Lily.

A boy in the line stuck his finger into the back of the boy in front of him—like a knife. "Ha! Her dad got held up!"

The boy in front laughed and raised his hands high in the air. "I surrender!" he yelped. "Help, help, I surrender!"

Even after they were gone, Lily's head buzzed.

~

All morning long, Gwen Vander Schaaf had been watching for Randall Decker. Which meant that by the time 11:45 rolled around, Randall seemed hours off the mark.

Suppose he'd picked Lily up at the back door? Suppose he'd already come and gone?

She trotted down the stairs, making a show of traveling toward the lunchroom. Lily was at the door, still. In coat and gloves and red wool cap. Gwen had meant to say something chipper and impressive as she passed, but the sight of that pale child rendered her speechless. She stopped. She laid her hand on the girl's forehead, guessing precisely what temperature she would find.

~

Before she could situate the girl in the sickroom, Gwen had to move the big bucket Mr. Menecke had set on the cot earlier in the day. To her relief, the bucket was dry. The brown cloud that bloomed on the ceiling high overhead appeared no larger than it had for the last umpteen years.

"It shouldn't be long," she told the girl. The sickroom held only the cot, a few chairs, the eye-test box with its scroll of paper E's multiplying, shrinking, facing this way and that. Gwen opened a flannel blanket at the foot of the cot. "Why don't you just lie down?"

The girl let Gwen help her off with her ratty coat and hat, her chalky white shoes. Gwen lifted one of the silvery braids, then set it back carefully. "You have hair just like your dad," she said.

The cot creaked as the girl lay down. "His hair's brown now," she said.

Gwen let loose a startled, hiccuping laugh. "Is that right? Your dad sat in front of me in homeroom, through high school. We were together most of elementary, too. He did cartoon voices. Daffy Duck and Bugs Bunny. To tell the truth, I think I was half in love with him!"

The declaration sounded like some amused admission Gwen

might have made a hundred times to a hundred different people—or, perhaps, like something she'd come up with at just this moment—but it traveled closer to the truth of the matter than Gwen had ever been before, and she shivered when she was through.

Lily narrowed her eyes at Gwen, as if trying to decide whether or not she was teasing, then rolled over on her side and stared at the wall.

The other children returned from lunch. Shoes scraped across floors as feet slid beneath desks. The hall grew quiet. The day settled into its after-lunch torpor. To Gwen's surprise and delight, Lily fell asleep.

Imagine that: Gwen sitting there beside a child who might almost have been her own! Imagine that. Gwen stared at the chalky whorls left on her fingertips by the girl's shoes, at the spot on the ceiling, puffed and brown as gingerbread. She picked up a book someone had left behind on the eye-test box. Nancy Drew. As a girl, Gwen had read Nancy Drew. She ran her fingers across the book's familiar felty paper. Nancy Drew. Off to Louisiana with pals Bess and George to solve the case of the haunted showboat.

As if an alarm went off—at one o'clock, when the sickroom door opened—Lily opened her eyes and sat up on the cot.

Gwen closed the book on her finger and stared. At Randall. Who looked like a peeled green twig, and wore a shrunken, orange sweater with diamonds of vinyl puckered across the front. Randall. Who said, "Sorry I'm late."

A hefty woman with the gray and greasy complexion of a slice of headcheese followed Randall into the room and plopped herself down in a folding chair by the door. The woman—the one from the newspapers—kicked off her pair of high heels with a clatter, then padded across the sickroom in her bare feet to dangle a roll of hard candies in front of Lily's face. "Candy, hon?"

The girl looked to Gwen as if for answer. Gwen said, "She was feeling sick to her stomach. She may have a fever."

Randall looked up at the ceiling. "A fever," he said. He sounded like a man who had just been told the price of an object; a man who wished to appear to weigh his desire for that object against its price, but did not, in fact, know the going rates. Randall sucked in his skinny cheeks. "I remember that spot on the ceiling, there," he said. "You"—he glanced over at Gwen—"didn't you and me go to school together? You remember that spot?"

Lily and Gwen looked at each other; almost involuntarily, Gwen reached down and squeezed the girl's hand. Lily squeezed back.

"Gwen Vander Schaaf," said Randall, and then—as if he referred to someone not present, perhaps even dead—"she was one of the pretty girls."

"Why, Randall!" Mrs. Kramer winked at Gwen like some mother who hoped a second party might forgive her child his rudeness. "Randall, the lady still *is* pretty!"

~

When they were gone, Gwen stepped up on the chair she'd been sitting in, and, on tiptoe, looked out the sickroom's high window. An unfamiliar view, but she got her bearings. There, beside a car—old, gray—Randall was taking off his orange sweater. Mrs. Kramer, and then Lily, climbed into the car, and disappeared behind the glare on the windshield.

The car moved off through town, past the co-op, the gas station and houses, and, finally, the Tasty Treat and the school bus barn. As it traveled over the rise by Yoder's farm, Gwen believed she had lost sight of the thing entirely, but then, squinting, she spotted it again—gray, shaped like a snail—climbing what she realized must be the ridge along Penn's orchard.

Penn's orchard. She hadn't thought of Penn's orchard in years.

She caught the car once more as it neared the stand of oaks beside the turnoff to Lily's grandparents' farm. And, again, as it rose up from what had to be the bridge over Salisbury Creek; but then something—wet, disagreeable—fell onto the top of Gwen's head and she jumped off the chair.

Grainy, tan, and white. Plaster from the rotten ceiling.

By the time she climbed back up on the chair, the brightness of the day had swallowed the car as neatly as it had the last bits of snow on the hillsides, and so she sat down wearily in the chair by the cot and she read on Nancy Drew in Louisiana: stolen cars and voodoo magic, broken hearts and grits and Spanish moss and ghosts in the bayou night. How empty such a story seemed to Gwen now, particularly when she knew that somehow or other an ending would be drummed up from all those bits and pieces, that nothing whatsoever would be left unexplained.

Thieves

THIS IS THE Dorans' house: sad, fake grandeur. Corinthian columns made from U.S. aluminum. You stand in the Dorans' front yard, you get the feeling the burlap hasn't rotted off the root balls of the little ashes and hackberries, in a hard wind they'll tilt like the buoys at the lake; and *inside* the house, someone seems, at every moment, night or day, to have just snapped on a light, especially in the kitchen. No doubt this has had an effect on Mrs. Doran, who's very sweet, but also a sort of constantly startled-looking alcoholic.

Blue is the color of Mrs. Doran's kitchen. Blue-blue. Like in the Bible stories they have at dentists' offices.

Mrs. Doran's blue kitchen is where my big sister Ann and Ann's boyfriend, the handsome Jimmy Doran, and I sit when the two golfers, in town for a tournament, walk in the Dorans' front door. The golfers don't bother to knock, and, from the way they look around the Dorans' mostly empty kitchen, I think maybe they expected loud music, a keg in the corner, many available girls, even chips, dip.

Does Jimmy Doran notice the way confusion tweaks the corners of these golfers' mouths and sends their shoulders *up?* Not a bit. Jimmy's mom and dad are out of town for the weekend, and he's king of this air-conditioned plantation. Jimmy says to the golfers, in his sultry way, "Hey, man, hey." Jimmy has his good points, but news of his attractions got back to him at an early age and led to a number of creepy habits, one being this slow escape of drugged greetings between his showy teeth—white, everywhere, a regular operating room of teeth.

"How you doing, Jim?" says the first golfer. *Tall.* Has to *duck* so he won't hit the ceiling lamp, that's how tall the first golfer happens to be.

"Hey, man," Jimmy says once more, and smiles at the tall golfer, and smiles some more. The tall golfer, Dane, and his buddy, Rex— shorter, burly—they smile, too. Rex extends his smile to me, lets it inch around the room and lap its way up my legs, etc., but nobody can hold a smile as long as Jimmy. Although it's also true that no one could ever say whether Jimmy's really happy to see them, or if he's just doing Jimmy Doran's idea of what that might be like, or he's just thrilled by what jerks the rest of us are.

I mean, is *he* ridiculous, or is this ridicule, you see?

"So, where's the party?" asks the shorter golfer, Rex.

Ann smiles at the golfers like they're old friends. "Jim-*my,*" she says, "what'd you tell these guys?" Ann's particularly skinny these days, which makes her confident and energetic and sexy in the right kind of way, unlike myself, who inspires boys like Rex to stare, not at just my face, but at my breasts, too, and my neck, and my thighs, as if I'm maybe the next course, and would somebody hurry up and clear, please?

Jimmy laughs and hops and glides on the counter like a chimpanzee. "Dane!" he says. Smoke comes out between his fingers as he puffs and pulls on his Luckies. He begins a crazy explanation of how he *meant* to have a party, Dane man, but then—his eyes crackle with mischief, for a moment he's the cute little kid from a family TV show—hey, then he realized that he and old Dane here would probably just want to discuss the many happy times they knew at their alma mater, ha, ha, ha.

The tall golfer, Dane, shakes his head. He twists his big jaw this way and that. His hair is that dried-blood sort of red, and the day at the tournament burned him good. Where his sunglasses sat, there's a white mask, very precise; you can even see where the bow was thickest! And his arms— You look at this Dane, you want to sort of draw into yourself, not just because you don't want to bump his sunburn, but, also, the burn, and just how irritated he seems . . . well, maybe a person that tall would always look scary.

Dane lifts one of his big hands. He wears an enormous ring, gold, with a big red stone. He checks out his watch for the second time since he walked in the door. "Can I have a word with you, Jim?" he says.

Until this afternoon, when Jimmy set up tonight, Ann and I had never heard of Dane; it seems he knew Jimmy last year, in Phoenix, Arizona, where both spent twelfth grade at a private high school for wealthy and troublemaking kids.

"An intimate evening, Dane man," murmurs Jimmy. Dane pops a beer. For about one millionth of a second, he looks down at me over the top of his can, and he's got his mouth sort of screwed up, like we're boyfriend and girlfriend and we're in the middle of a fight. As if he is, in fact, my own true love, whose name I cannot say. He is a secret and my parents would murder me if they knew—

Crazy, this Dane. Intriguing. But certainly not a boy for me; though, having found love to be both exciting and terrible, I *do* keep my eyes open for better prospects at all times. Still, Dane here is like one of the young entrepreneurs who come by our house to try to get Dad to back, say, Italian restaurants or the manufacture of plastic pipes. Both Dane and Rex—his name, I swear, I have no intention of protecting the innocent—both wear golf pants, and Rex wears what Ann and I call a "Perry Como sweater," after a singer our Grandma Kaiser likes. Rex could actually be one of those bamboozler guys who turn up in strips like *Mary Worth* and *Judge Parker*. The cartoonists give the guys the wrong cars, wrong lapels, wrong names, and you know the code and it means: creep.

Ann gives me a quick look. Whom did we expect? Oh, handsome, intelligent delinquents from good families who would look—just *crazed* by a crazy afternoon spent with irons and woods or whatever you call them.

Jimmy frowns at Ann and me, like maybe he expects a mutiny. "Now Ann here's my hometown honey, Dane, ha, ha, ha!" he says. He yanks Ann over to the spot where he sits on the counter and takes a chomp on her shoulder blade.

"Ow!" Ann says. She follows this with a blurt of laughter, but anybody can see the bite hurt.

"Jimmy!" I say.

Jimmy smiles. Ann shakes her head. "It's okay, Clare. Shh."

"And Clare, there, is Ann's little sister."

"Ah," say the golfers, and just like that—so *that* was the boulder in the road: which one of us belonged to Jimmy?—just like that they turn to me.

"Jesus, Doran," says Rex, "the *little* sister?"

"Fourteen," says Jimmy. Quite proud. Like he grew me himself, I'm this year's prize pumpkin. "And smart, too!"

"Fourteen!" says Rex. "How can she be fourteen?"

I pretend I don't hear a thing. I plunk down, red-faced, on the linoleum and pat the back of the Dorans' schipperke, Dino. Dino is old and fat and smelly, but he's all right. He turns his head toward me when I pet him. He watches me with his milky old eyes, like he wants me to know he's appreciative.

"Fourteen!" says Rex.

Dane presses his hand down on the back of Rex's neck. "Knock it off, Rex," he says.

For a moment, nobody says anything, it's awful, but then Rex sort of laughs. "Okay, okay, I get the picture," he says. "I go check out the *TV Guide*, right?"

When I can bear to look up again, Rex stands with his back to the rest of us, helping himself to expensive scotch from the Dorans' liquor cabinet. Once, Ann told me this sad story about a time she and Jimmy hunted all over the Dorans' for a bag of coke they'd hidden while they were high; they kept finding pints of rotgut booze in places in which they thought only *they* would have been messed up enough to stick something, like the thirty-cup coffeemaker and a bag of that grass people use in Easter baskets.

"Scotch, anyone?" Rex asks.

No one even answers. Jimmy and Ann are whispering furiously. Dane—he kind of squints out into the dining room, as if being in the Dorans' kitchen hurts his eyes, too. He's taller than anyone I've ever been near in real life, with legs so long that, from where I am, down here on the floor, he seems almost distorted, like a retarded person, like his head will be too small when you finally get there.

After a while, he looks down at me. "Clare," he says. "What kind of name is that?"

Poor old Dino starts to act gross if you pet him too long, so, very fast, I have to get up off the floor, and this Dane rears back, like he thinks maybe I'll wrap my legs around his waist the way Dino wraps my embarrassed calf. Though isn't that, in fact, what Dane does want? Oh, who knows what goes on in the minds of boys? They want you because they hate you, they hate you because they want you.

I brush Dino away. I look out the open window over the Dorans' sink. Moths tap the screen, and june bugs. Our neighbors at our lake house have a machine that electrocutes every bug that likes its blue glow. All night: zzzzip!

"Clare means 'bright,'" I tell Dane, "'illustrious.'"

He reaches around me and closes the window. "Air-conditioning's on," he says, a little stern. That's who he is, but let *me* say, immediately, though Dane makes me mostly sick, still, I would like to have his admiration, and I don't think that's entirely unfair: I didn't miss the fact that he wrinkled his nose when Jimmy said I was smart, that he swallowed my supposedly very pretty face in one bite, and no doubt will begin working his way down soon. *And* he's a guy, he's big, he plays golf and looks like it. Compared with Dane, I may as well be one of those blurry photographs of missing kids they put on the back of milk cartons, right?

Actually, everything would be better if I were in love with a golfing entrepreneur-type like Dane instead of the person I do love (twenty, unreliable, this summer crisscrossing North America, lugging people's furniture and books and dishes from out of their old houses and, then, a few days later, into their new ones). My father could set a husband like Dane up manufacturing mobile homes or some necessary computer part. I could skip high school and take the GED. . . .

So *try*, I think. You could at least try!

I try. I let my eyes soften. I listen to the nervous, picked-up beat of my heart. That's love! Listen: Love! Love! Oooh, you're in love!

Well, this feels like holding your breath, you can't do it very long without knowing you're about to suffer irreversible damage.

Dane smiles at my shoulders. Should I see if he likes lasagna and antipasto, or has an interest in, maybe, the construction business, or tell him that Ann and I started golf lessons once? What happened to our golf lessons, anyway? Mother decided she didn't really want to drive us in from the lake house to the club, or maybe it was our own fault. Summer before last, Ann and I went to this ritzy camp, and, believe it or not, out of all those kids, Ann won Honor Camper, and I, Achievement Camper, which meant Ann was friendliest and I was willing to try the most things; but what do either of us really know how to do? Take the tennis court at our lake house: no one in our family knows how to use it. "I want to see you girls out there playing tennis!" says Dad. A sad bully. He doesn't play, Mom doesn't play, but it's a good idea, we agree, and out we go that very afternoon because we want to make him happy. We want to exercise our bodies, don't we? In the slamming sunlight, we laugh at the crazy balls and the red haze that floats over everything green, but the fact of the matter is, we don't last. We stagger back into the big house overlooking the lake, our dock with the unused water and three kinds of boats, and we drink Diet Pepsi and think of funny things to say about the people on *Oprah*. The truth, in my opinion, is that Ann and I don't know how to do anything worthwhile except read good books, and even that may turn out not to be an accomplishment:

Look at Ann over there, so marvelously skinny and tan, but also choking, wriggling in one of Jimmy Doran's almost-wrestling holds. I know what she would say if I interfered: "Don't interfere, Clare!" And who does she imagine she is? Anna Karenina today? Madame Bovary tomorrow?

And me? I read William Blake and imagine myself sheltered in the caves of peaceful golden lions; or maybe I'm *Green Mansions'* lovely and mysterious Rima, always racing ahead of my true love, who will go mad with grief at my death, and carry my bones with him all his days so we two may be buried in one tomb.

"You came in first today, huh, Dane?" says Jimmy, smiling, a little breathless from his struggle with Ann. Dane nods, but also appears concerned for Ann. This makes me think better of him. "Rex came out okay, too," he says.

Jimmy winks at me over Ann's bobbling head, as if to say, *Aren't you glad you're spending the evening with this modest guy who won the golf tournament?*

I know better than to even pretend to be pleased; how Jimmy would spring at the throat of any real joy on my part isn't worth thinking about. He likes me dispirited. I'm the sort of isolationist he wishes Ann would be. Or he *says* he wishes that. Really, he loves Ann, there's just something wrong with him. Jimmy—he's like the people who have to be wheeled around school; when you do something nice for them, they want to give you a pat on the arm, but their hand flies out and, instead, they poke you in the eye.

Rex holds up the scotch again. "Drinks?" he says.

Ann laughs over her shoulder, escapes into the Dorans' powder room, probably to make herself vomit the grilled cheese and chili she ate before Jimmy picked us up. Personally, I wouldn't enjoy a meal I meant to throw up, but Annie's lucky in this regard.

"I guess I'll just have a beer," I tell Rex.

"*Beer?*" says Rex, and then Dane moves closer to me, and then, *bang,* I say something obscene about scotch, a word I wouldn't ordinarily say, just because I know boys like these cannot abide such a word from a girl.

"So," says Dane, "a toilet mouth."

"Ha! Little Clare!" says Jimmy Doran. He falls over on his side, laughing.

Ann throws up in the Dorans' powder room. I check out the guys to see if they heard, but they just start talking about Dane's golf scholarship to Arizona State in the fall. Ann does it again. Rex says he knows a guy Jimmy knows. "That's right," says Jimmy.

Ann has promised me she isn't anorexic or anything, and it is true that she eats lots of good salads, and hard-boiled eggs, which supposedly burn more calories than they contain.

I couldn't eat another hard-boiled egg to save my life. I weigh 118. Oh, guys act like they love it, they just spatter me with deranged compliments—lust and disgust—when Ann and I go down the street, but I know: at five foot five, I am already eight pounds beyond okay. I look at my mother and see myself headed toward skirted swimsuits and vertical stripes, fast, no resources but willpower and a shaky promise of one hundred hits of speed from a kid at school.

Sure, Jimmy and the golfers say. And, *All right!* But eventually sports and mutual acquaintances fail them, they're high and dry.

Dane sort of laughs and leans forward on the counter, spreads his big fingers out there like something we might cook up if we get hungry. "So Jim," he says, "we're an odd number here, did you notice that?"

"I should have known it was going to be love at first sight for you and Clare!" Jimmy says. "Ha, ha, ha!" Then he digs his car keys from his jeans, swings them in his usual menacing and energetic way, and, just like that, he's out the door.

Ann wobbles into the kitchen, pale, stricken.

"Are you okay?" I whisper.

Her breath is sweet and sharp, toothpaste and bile. "I know where he went," she says miserably. "To get Micki Traub for Rex."

To make Ann feel better, I pretend to gag in revulsion. I don't know Micki Traub, but would recognize her on the street. She's pretty in a murky way, like ladies you see on the news, scurrying down the streets of Iran, dusky brows, dusky lashes.

"Annie." I follow her into the Dorans' front hall. We both know Jimmy sometimes stops by the houses of Micki and other girls after sleeping with Ann, but Ann always treats it as fresh news; in the dark, her skinny face is shadowy, like a skeleton. It makes me want to cry, to see her so sad. "Don't worry, honey," I say.

Ann looks out the door. She says, "Go away, Clare."

I shake my head. When I first saw the face of my true love, I felt I'd been hit by a poisoned dart, and I was falling, falling through leaves and branches. I didn't give him my heart; love and beauty *stole* it, and I don't, as they say in books, suffer the loss gladly. Which means nobody admires me for my love, not him, not anyone. But at least I don't rattle when I walk. I am, even, a virgin still, though no one believes it—that the battle makes me carry my intact thing like a shield before me each time I meet my love.

"Another beer, Clare?" Rex calls from the kitchen. Such a bright blue square, that kitchen, when you stand out in the dark hall. The kitchen at our house is white. White enamel pots hanging on white walls. White tile, white grout. When a guest asks for a glass of red wine at our house, my mother winces.

Somehow—I think because it takes so long for Jimmy to return—Ann agrees with Rex that we ought to play strip poker. Down she sits on the living room carpet, laughing, like we're old hands at this game, which she has played exactly once, with the girls in Cochise Cabin at Camp Potawatomi, and I have played exactly never.

"Ann," I say. She gives me a secret, ferocious look. "Well," I say, "as long as I can quit whenever I want ..."

Ann and Rex laugh. "Sit down and play," says Dane.

I think Rex takes off his pants first in order to keep his soft belly covered by his shirt. This makes me sorry for him. I look away, at the Dorans' carpet—pale green—and the chrome legs of the coffee table, and Dino looking up at me through the table's glass top. Rex's pants make a slippery, grown-up noise as they fall, like Dad's pants when we were little and all had to stay together in motel rooms on trips.

I smile across the circle, hoping to cheer Ann when she loses her shirt, but *my* Ann has gone off, the way she's been able to since we were kids, and this other Ann acts as if we're strangers. She slaps her knees and laughs at Rex's moronic jokes, she gives *me* a creepy look when I have no choice but to remove my own blouse.

Fast, I yank it off. I don't want anyone to think I imagine myself provocative in my sturdy white bra, this thing made for grown-up women with large breasts, which must make me look like a lewd nurse, repellent with creepy desires.

Rex rocks back onto his elbows, laughing, at something Ann whispers to him. Dino takes this as a call for affection and, ever faithful, slowly gets to his tired feet, tacks in the direction of Rex's head, and gives Rex a little lick on the nose.

"Yuck, man!" says Rex, and sits right up. Rex wears boxer shorts of baby blue. That's all. "Here, you dumb pooch," he says, and pours half of his drink into an ashtray. "Here you go, you dumb old pooch."

He's startled when I snatch the ashtray away, but, oh, Dane, loony confusion lights *his* face, and, yes, I've seen it before, on other boys. First they believe I'm a kind of dartboard at which to aim a triple-X fantasy. Then something makes them see I'm human, and they feel just terribly noble because of this change of vision. Then they think *I'm* noble. And isn't it grand?

You might imagine I want to kick Dane in the teeth, but that loony look feels better than the other, and I'm a little moved myself. I feel pretty okay as I stand at the kitchen sink, dumping scotch and water down the Dorans' disposal. Maybe I do love Dane after all. Maybe my love for my true love is only a deep infatuation, something childish and never capable of maturity.

"Ah-hem! Miss Clare!" says Jimmy, entering the kitchen through the garage entrance. The shadowy Micki is behind him, smiling. Jimmy must have shut off his engine a way up the street, just hoping to catch us doing something stupid. Like playing strip poker, maybe.

"Fetching wardrobe, Clare!" says Jimmy.

I remain cool. All of us do. We have to with Jimmy dancing around us, laughing, his hands on his cheeks like he's shocked, my, my, my, while we put on our clothes, and act like, *Well, yeah, we finished up that game, so let's just get dressed.*

"Are you working at Hy-Vee this summer, Micki?" asks Ann as she steps into her pants. As normal as if they meet in the hall at school. Believe it or not, the two of them do have a kind of relationship. Whenever Ann and Jimmy break up, Ann calls his newest flame and—in order to keep tabs on Jimmy—offers advice on how to handle him. She has become, amazingly, an instant best friend to confused blondes and brunettes all over town. Crazy, but in a week, three at the most, Jimmy's back, he never left. I think sometimes the girls miss Ann more than Jim.

"Gee, I'm glad I was off work tonight," Micki says.

Rex nods. He's happy as a lark with Micki. And Dane's happy, too. "Here," he says, and, with big fingers, fixes my earring—unclasped during all the dressing and undressing—and smooths his hand down my back, and, without even asking if I want one, gets me a beer.

I say hi to Micki, as if we know each other, because I don't want her to feel like I think I'm better than she is. I do, of course. Not on purpose, but I do. All day long: greater than, less than. Like in math class. When I think of that, I think of seventh grade, when Mr. Kuhn put a lot of different mathematical symbols and their meanings on the bulletin board, and he included those two tipped-over Vs, Greater Than, Less Than, and then somebody drew nipples on the points of the Vs, and then, a few days later, somebody else wrote beneath them: "I don't know, we look about the same size to me!"

"Well, what about SMU?" says Micki Traub to Rex, having what I'm afraid she imagines a kind of elevated, collegiate conversation: UCLA. UNM. UCSD.

"Stop that!" Ann says to Jimmy, but this time I don't look to see why. Dane's big arm lies on my shoulder, hot as a loaf of bread, and I'm thinking, What's next? Politely, I ask, "You're sure you're not dying, Dane? I can feel the heat from your burn."

Dane is impressed. He holds his fingers at various distances above his skin, gauging temperatures.

"Well, how about NYU then?" Micki Traub says to Rex.

"Or XYZ?" I whisper to Dane. "LMNOP?"

Dane looks down at me, confused, then a startled blurt of laughter shoots out of his mouth: "Ha!"

Micki Traub turns. I feel bad. I wait for her to say something awful, but she just taps my shoulder. "I've seen you at games. You have the prettiest hair."

"Thank you," I say. Under any circumstance, a compliment tends to do me in, and at the moment I feel like a heel, which means my voice warbles all over the place. Ann frowns. She hates it when I get like this so I stick my head into the refrigerator and pretend to look for a lime.

Jimmy winks at the rest of us after Micki and Rex head for the family room. At that moment, he reminds me of his dad, a well-known lech of a lawyer who supposedly tries to put it to his clients whenever possible.

"I can't believe you brought that bitch!" says Ann.

"Oh, Christ," Jimmy says, "her neck's even dirty! She looks like she spent the day rolling in the newspaper! What do you care about her?"

"Jimmy!" Ann laughs into her hands. "Not so loud!"

"Come on," Dane says, and with his hand on the back of my neck starts me moving toward the front hall.

"Here." He points to the bottom step of the stairs leading up to the Dorans' bedrooms. "We can talk here."

It's all the same to me. Basically, a boy will steer you toward dark and some sort of horizontal surface, though vertical will do, too, if you have dark.

"So what do people do for fun around here?" he asks.

I laugh, I shrug. Nobody except Ann and my friend Maureen ever talks about anything of interest to me. Maureen and I each have copies of *Sonnets from the Portuguese* and *The English Romantic Poets* and we read poems to each other over the phone. We agree that if we were boys we would be so nice to our girlfriends.

Every once in a while, a car drives by the house, its lights tracking the ground like the hound dogs in cartoons. Dane says some stuff about Jimmy and Phoenix, and how Jimmy screwed girls right and left at Briarly Academy, and that he was the one who told Jim—in a letter to Ann, which upset our household for a good week—to put a line through "Love" at the end, and close "Sincerely."

While Dane talks, I twist the big red and gold ring on his big finger around and around. I think that ring might be very nice, the ring of my boyfriend Dane, worn on a gold chain around my neck to show I love him so.

"What are you thinking about?" Dane asks me.

"Oh, negative capability," I say.

Dane laughs. He leans close to me, I think for a kiss, but instead he pushes my hair behind my ears. "That girl liked your hair, but she's a skag," he says. "You shouldn't wear it the way you do. You should wear it this way."

I laugh to conceal how pained I am at such correction. The *ease* with which boys tell girls what to do, and after we spend half of our days trying to think of ways to please them! Once, I had a pimple on my cheek, and, as we said good-bye, my true love said to me, "Get rid of that before next time, okay, baby?"

"Hey!" Jimmy and Ann start when they come around the corner and find Dane and me talking on the stairs.

"What time is it?" I ask with a yawn.

"Not even ten," says Ann, and runs with Jimmy up to his bedroom.

"You're not going to fall asleep on me, are you?" says Dane. "Here. Stand up. Come on!"

I stand on the first step, but no, says Dane, you have to be higher.

His eyes don't have any color in the dark. This happens to my real love's eyes, all boys' eyes, in the dark. How much black and white and gray time I have spent with boys this past year, talking and then kissing and then struggling!

When I stand on the third step, this Dane kisses me. It's okay. Even if it weren't okay, what would I do? I kiss Dane back. "All right," he says, as if we've struck a bargain, and he lifts me into the air, and he carries me upstairs—the first person to pick me up in ages. Though it certainly does not feel like being carried used to: end of the night, pajamas, sweet sleep.

Dane carries me right into the dark of Mr. and Mrs. Dorans' bedroom and places me, and himself, on the pale island of their bed in one movement.

"Well, hey!" I say, and sit up and swing my legs over the edge.

Dane pulls me down. The bed is stripped. A loose mattress button pokes into my angel wing. After a little while, Dane stands up. "Stay there," he says, and unzips his pants—zip—and they fall in the same whispery way that Rex's did, earlier.

A tremendous amount of Dane covers that suddenly small double bed: long pale legs covered with a roof of puffy hair, like dandelions when they're at the blowing stage; and arms, half white, half dark with the burn; and the big dark face, and his feet sticking over the end. I've never been in bed with anyone, just in my true love's car, where everything is close up, hard to see, and even reach. Because of Dane's sunburn, I feel bad about the usual scuffle. "Sorry," I say.

Dane takes courtesy as encouragement, pins one of my arms above my head with new determination.

"Don't be fourteen," he says between clenched teeth.

"I *am* fourteen," I say. "And I'm keeping my underwear on, too!"

You know all the things he says; if I tell you, he'll sound more stupid than he is, and I'll sound more conceited than he'll sound stupid.

Because he asks and asks, I do touch his penis for one second. A penis is soft and silky and sort of a friendly little pup, but this is an entire area I don't get: Are some people really interested in the parts of others except as those parts can give themselves pleasure? I mean, my true love acts very excited when he means to excite me, but isn't it the prospect of his own possible pleasure that excites him? I'm *happy* to make him happy and when he kisses my breasts, sometimes I want to weep with pained joy, almost the creepy way I feel like crying when something terribly corny happens, like they crown beauty queens or play the national anthem, but is this what people mean?

After what must be hours of grappling—my lips puffed, chin scraped—Dane drops one of his long arms over the side of the bed. His fingers scrabble around on the carpet for a minute, then he brings up his watch. "I guess we better go downstairs," he says, quiet, lots of sighs. Like my parents when they feel let down: "We see you've lost all interest in the piano, Clare." Or, "I guess a trip to the most beautiful beaches in the world wasn't special enough for you, hmm, Clare?"

Downstairs, Dane and I sit on the living room couch, in the dark, not talking. Mentally, I connect the flag pole of a motorboat parked in the neighbor's drive and the trellis of another neighbor and the Dorans' yard light: an isosceles triangle.

"Well," Dane says, finally breaking the silence, "what if I gave you my ring?"

"What?"

"My ring. Would you like to have it?"

I smile as if he doesn't mean it, really, because maybe he doesn't mean it, really.

He shakes his head. "Would you like me to come back again next week, anyway?"

"Oh!" I say. I sound just like my mother. "That would be nice, wouldn't it?"

"Hey, Dane." Rex stands in the doorway, Micki Traub leaning into him. They both look happy, worn. Rex does a little golf swing in the air. "Got to get going, buddy-o. Long way to Des Moines."

Like we're all set to the same clock, at just that moment, Ann and Jimmy come downstairs, too.

"Hey!" Jimmy claps his hands. "Did everybody make sure they didn't leave any evidence for my poor, old, weak-hearted mother to find?"

"I'll make sure," I whisper to Dane, relieved to get away. But then Jimmy says, "Uh-oh!" very stagey, like he's just remembered something incriminating himself, and up the stairs he pounces after me, and grabs hold of me in the hall.

"So what happened with Dane?" he whispers.

I shake my head. Jimmy knows me well enough to see I feel lousy. He brings his face close to mine and kisses me on the forehead. Then the cheek. Like I'm the most fragile thing in the world, and his lips are little powder puffs. I don't know whether he's being brotherly or what. Half the time when Ann leaves the two of us alone in a room, Jimmy teases me about my true love, and the other half of the time he tries to kiss me. "Come on over here, Clare," he'll murmur, or he'll haul himself across the carpet to me on his knees, whatever. I'm sorry, but yes, I sometimes do kiss him. Mostly because I feel embarrassed for him. He really looks like he might cry when you say no. And you can see he figures he *has* to try to kiss you, so imagine the mess you get in when he's kneeling at your feet, and the TV is on, and you can't quite hear when Ann's coming back, and all he really wants is one kiss, please.

"Dane didn't hurt you or anything, did he, Clare?"

"He didn't hurt me," I say, "but I don't ever want to see him again."

Jimmy nods. "That's all I want to know. You're my kind of girl, Clare, you know? You're really the one."

"Jimmy," I say, "you are hopeless."

"I am, aren't I?" Jimmy says. "No, that's not right! I'm *hopeful,* and *you're* hopeless, Clare!"

I don't laugh. I am tired to death of being misunderstood by not just strangers but the people who know me best, and I say, "It just so happens, Jimmy, that I've always believed things were about to get better soon."

Jimmy nods. For a minute, I feel a little lurch of sympathy between us, but then he starts coming at me again with those lips, and this time I just move away, and I whisper, "Don't do that, Jim. You don't have to do that."

You would expect him to make wide eyes of surprise. He does. He laughs. "Clare, Clare," he says, and pats my cheek and hops and skips down the hall, and then back down the stairs.

Mr. and Mrs. Doran's room is very different with the light on: before, with Dane, it was a pool of dark, an island of mattress, but now it's filled with matching pieces of furniture and crispy curtains and creamy graduation photos of Jimmy and his beautiful big sister, Margaret. I sit down on the mattress. My feet dangle over the edge as if I'm a footsore pilgrim sitting on the edge of a river.

"Oh, Clare!" The people downstairs call up to me, in a silly chorus: "Oh, Clare!" Then they all laugh, and do it again: "Oh, Clare!"

I roll onto my stomach. I dig my chin into the cool blue fabric of the mattress and, like an old dog, stare straight ahead.

Woof.

A little bottle sits on the bedside table: "Rx," says its label. "Good for One Laugh." Across the bottom, a cartoon doctor chases a cartoon nurse, her mouth open in a tiny black scream. The bottle contains M&M candies. I eat one as I read the gilt message looped across a photograph perched on the table: Season's Greetings from the Dorans in 1970!"

It's plain that the tiny children in the photo are Jimmy and Margaret, but even so it takes me a minute to straighten out the fact that the pretty woman who holds the kids is not the grown-up beautiful Margaret I have met, but Jimmy's young mother. Also, back then, *Mr.* Doran wore a mustache and a look of happy expectancy, both of which strike me almost as a disguise, something meant to throw off viewers of the future.

But, then, I suppose that's who he really was in those days, and I would like to warn him, and her, this sweet young mom and dad, "Look out, get serious now before it's too late!" but it's already too late.

I screw the lid back on the bottle. My fingers feel stiff and thick, as if I've suddenly grown a layer of bark. History, I think. I will look back at this night someday and hold myself accountable. I will say, as if I were someone else entirely, almost my own parent, "What on earth were you doing?"

This scares me, because *I* won't be there to answer, and I *know* the answer, right now, which is:

What was I doing? Don't you remember? I was doing the best that I could.

English as a Second Language

T HE FIRST STORE is no convenience market, no, not one of those weary laugh-getters of our time, symbols of the fast-paced nothing for something. The first store is old. Customers track in the snow, and the melt swells the wood floors to the dark, leaf-mold stain of footpaths in forests. Mousetraps and vegetable scubbers pinned to cardboards hang over the store entrance. Packed snow in the vestigial parking lot. It creaks when the man drives in, when he stops.

Crocker: his name.

Slick-bottomed shoes uncertain beneath him, Crocker crosses the lot, enters the above unnamed muggy store, and, with only a few turns of his head, locates the pastry racks. Fruit pies. Doughnuts in boxes shaped like tiny houses, blue curtains printed on either side of the cellophane picture windows.

Crocker does not buy doughnuts.

Crocker selects a see-through package of twin devil's food cakes, coconut-coated and shaped like small igloos. Crocker chooses white coconut for the modicum edge of dignity it holds over pink; believe me, he knows this is not much.

Outside again, he carries his paper bag a little in front of him so that he may not appear furtive.

A teacher. English as a Second Language. Large high school. Overworked, underpaid.

In his rusty car, as he drives, Crocker wrestles the pastries from their wrappers, takes a first bite. Really, he disapproves of them as much as anyone does. He knows their signals; made by an enormous company that does not care for the inventive, perishable life of the individual, the pastries are a puff of corporate America. Eating them is, in a sense, suicidal. And doesn't their comic-book ring of sweet and goo only *remind* one of something genuinely tasty, thus demonstrating how far from actual goodness we might stand and still move jaws, swallow?

A brand name for an article of food. Funny, and spreading. Chicken and bananas—whole in their various skins—might now appear the brainchildren of corporations named Country Pride and Dole.

Just the week before, the mother of Jesus Aguasvivas— Dominican, no English at all—brought an exquisite coconut pudding to the ESL potluck. Crocker took three servings, entirely too much, and only guilt stopped his taking a fourth. "*Gordo,*" Crocker said to Mrs. Aguasvivas: fat. He patted his belly, and waited for the woman to say no, no. But she only laughed, held up her fingers in a small measure. "*Gordito,*" she said. A little fat.

Despite Crocker's protests, Jesus left his mother alone at the potluck: a small woman, smiling, folding and refolding a piece of aluminum foil. Jesus spent the evening with his hairdo—complicated, spray-stiffened—in front of the locker room's bright bank of mirrors.

What Crocker meant to do was to help people open a channel between themselves and others. Community. Fraternity. Instead, his best efforts trot off to the marketplace, enter into the service of compact disc sales, steamy bar dates at places with names like Beef on the Hoof.

"They don't take anything seriously," he told his wife. "They think life here is one big amusement park and all you need is money for the rides." This was an exaggeration, of course, and though Crocker's wife knew Crocker to be a good man, she scolded him: "So go ahead and change jobs!" A smart and pretty woman, his wife has grown snappish. On that occasion, to show her exasperation, she threw the magazine in her lap at a foundering dracaena by the window. The distorted plant looked otherworldly to Crocker, like something out of the Dr. Seuss books of his little son.

"Did you think their lives would be one long barn-raising and potluck supper?" the wife asked. The look on her face was shrewd, appraising, something honed on the stonier parts of their marriage. "What's with you, anyway? Look at how you dress lately! Are you trying to be a model of worldly renunciation or what?"

~

Like a shedding dog or a snowstorm, the coconut pastries make a mess all over Crocker's sports jacket and car. He never ate these products as a child. He ridiculed them! His mother educated him in excellent pies under roofs of melted Vermont cheddar; a mother who baked Brownies Cockaigne so dense with chocolate and sugar and butter that they resembled the mud desserts Crocker (then a boy) once made in his backyard.

Coconut everywhere.

Coconut in his graying mustache, the cracks of upholstery.

With a jerk, Crocker stops at a car wash and in its gloomy parking lot he vacuums the seats, the carpet. He stomps his feet on the creaking snow and vacuums himself, too.

His wife would never in a million years guess that he might stop (stoop) to eat these pastries. What does his wife know about him, after all? She pays close attention to the child, a beauty of two with blond curls and every movement a dance, and for this Crocker is happy; but he also sometimes feels that he should have killed himself or entered the Peace Corps while there was still a chance, back when particular people did not need him quite so much.

As Crocker left the house this morning, his wife sounded both weepy and peremptory. "You come home *right* after you run tonight!"

(Around and around the dirt floors beneath the high school, alone in that panicky miners' dark, the ceiling lit only here and there with incandescents. He might have been on the lam in a future, subterranean world, running from something inexorable in its hunger.)

Mr. Fitness, his wife calls him, and it is true, even in high school, back in the days when no one ran except members of track teams, Crocker put on his grays, regularly, and ran to a neighboring burg, a round trip of fifteen miles. Other kids drove past, some kicking up slush and laughing, but most rooting on what he knew they considered bizarre behavior. In college, he kept at it even during that period when he wore hair so long it cupped at his shoulders and he resembled Buster Brown. He cut weight for the wrestling team while windowpane acid and his very own brain caused the fishnet hung from his ceiling to cast an entirely new order of shadow over the world. Somewhere in the duplex he shares with wife and son, there exists a maple rung from a dorm room chair that is pocked with the teeth marks of his former zeal. His wife believes the thing a memento of a favorite dog, but many people from Crocker's past have offered up for the delectation of more recent acquaintances a tale of a crazy, starving wrestler who paced dormitory halls, chewing on a piece of wood and spitting into a paper cup.

In three days, Crocker will be thirty-nine years old.

He no longer dreams the dreams he could share with everyone he knew, dreams in which he must take a test in a class he never attended, or perform in a play for which he has not learned the lines. Worse, he now wakes terrified, sweating, and longs to cry out like his little son: Daddy! Mommy! The other night, his son awoke crying just this, and—not yet aroused by his own terrors, still half-asleep, terrified—Crocker sat up in bed, heart drumming for that cry in the distance. With hallucinogenic clarity, bare planets—rocks—hurtled through space, and Crocker was out there with them, and he knew as if he were God: There are no mothers and fathers.

"Daddy, Dad!" the child cried again.

And then Crocker settled back into his soul, became a father once more, took shape as if called into being by desire.

~

Beneath the driver's seat lies a fuzzed and sticky can-opener. Crocker nudges the repellent thing farther into the dark with the car wash vacuum, unaware that the opener pushes his missing chrome pen, too; the pen edges beneath a newspaper Crocker once saved. The newspaper features an article on one of Crocker's Vietnamese students and her family. The article tells, among other things, how Dep was forced to watch her mother and a younger sister be raped, thrown into the sea, devoured by sharks.

Why he saved the article Crocker no longer remembers. Some testament to the awful world? Or survival? A reminder that what private perversity invents to rack his own nights has no weight when poised beside the memories of others?

Dep in class today—silent, silent, her conversational partner waiting—and then: "She my best friend, but I never forget her."

Crocker has abandoned the outmoded grammar drills; a good thing, yet sometimes the sluggish flow of student invention drives him to distraction. This morning, he corrected the girl, "That's 'and,' Dep, not 'but.'"

However, didn't an unvoiced thought make Dep's "but" sensible? *I know I will never see my best friend again, but I will never forget her.*

He ought to apologize, really. For knowing what the girl meant but asking for greater precision.

And asking for greater precision?

And *still* asking for greater precision.

Sometimes, Crocker wonders if Dep might be a grown woman, not a girl at all: a small woman in a high school full of big kids.

Once upon a time, this Dep had eight brothers and sisters; and, more important, a place in an immortal chain of ancestral graves and rice fields. For a good long while—lacking a Vietnamese equivalent for the word "I"—Dep referred to herself as "your student." These days, she resides in a county youth home, a yellowing building that appears to have been gnawed upon by its residents: besides Dep, five American girls and two American boys, all of whom either ran away from home or were kicked out.

"Do you practice your English at dinner?" Crocker once asked. Dep shook her head emphatically. Her shiny, chin-length hair flew out from her head and slapped at her cheeks. "They monsters," she whispered. Crocker nodded in sympathy. He told her a story of how, once, after traveling home from college, he sat down at the supper table with his own nine brothers and sisters, and no one even noticed his presence.

Dep smiled into her hands. "Maybe, Mista Crocka, no one notice you gone!" she said.

Quite a bit of time passed before Crocka, understood that the girl did not tease him; that her words would be taken for comfort in her world, where the family made a circle that went around and around and around.

~

"Crocker!" Behind him, parked in the glare of one of the car wash stalls, two of his students—Pakistani brothers. The younger one, nicknamed Pop, waves from the backseat of a large red convertible; Ahmad smokes a cigarette and lolls against the car.

Do they know they must not begin to wash that car with its top down? What are they doing with the top down in this weather, anyway? And how could they possibly own such a car?

Crocker waves to the boys as he puts the vacuum hose back in place. He has gotten the best of the coconut, but feels absurd.

How could you redeem the world without putting out all human consciousness?

The sort of question that makes Crocker hungry.

"One minute!" he calls to the boys. "Wait one minute!"

A convenience market sits across the parking lot from the car wash, and Crocker walks rapidly in its direction.

Perhaps everyone feels vaguely criminal in a convenience market, where deterrence of crime affects everything: the layout, the friendliness masking raving suspicion, the lighting, the mirrors, the notes to potential robbers. Think of *that!* "Cashier keeps no more than twenty dollars in change. Cashier does not have access to safe."

"Quik," write Crocker's students. "Cheez." "Cum."

Ahmad and Pop. Initially, they entered Crocker's classes with bowed heads, wore wide-sleeved white shirts, stayed after unbidden to wipe the blackboards. Now they like tight denim and playing nasty tricks; they slyly deposit gobs of phlegm in the hair of studying classmates, knock over pails of cafeteria slops, put an occasional spin on the wheelchairs of handicapped kids.

Crocker carries two twin-packs of the coconut pastries to the counter. One each for the students, another for himself. And should neither boy want the fourth pastry, Crocker promises himself he will chuck the thing in a waste bin.

Behind the cash register, the face of the young clerk looks hot, like the faces of cafeteria workers, people bent over steam tables. "You don't ever want to get a job here," she says when Crocker approaches the counter. "I thought I was hired, but now I have to take a polygraph test. They want to know if I've ever done drugs!" She frowns in the direction of a pair of disembodied hands busily filling the refrigerator cases from the storeroom side: sandwiches and microwave burgers and individual, huge pickles packaged in brine and plastic. "I can forget it," she says.

Just to be friendly, Crocker says, "Maybe you don't have to take the test. Maybe it's not even legal."

The clerk looks him in the eye. Crocker hands her the pastries. "Those are really bad for you," the clerk says, before her particular circumstances once more shoot up before her like a torpedo from water, and she blurts, "They won't even let me wear jeans here! All I've got is jeans! No way am I going to last."

Crocker finds the clerk pretty in her despair and baby-blue pants. In a spill of harmless attraction, he says, "I hear we're hiring at the high school these days."

"Really?" The clerk straightens a frisky basket of matchbooks. Interestingly enough, her face becomes homely during its stab at mature consideration. "But look," she says, sighing and resuming her cute and cranky youth, "you probably have to go to college to teach and all."

Both of them turn in alarm as the back room's swinging doors pop, and out steps a young man, shrugging into an overcoat.

"I wish you wouldn't do that," says the clerk. The young man— clearly the manager—laughs. "See you tomorrow," he says.

Once the young man is gone, Crocker tells the clerk, "Actually, the jobs I was talking about at school . . . I meant jobs in the cafeteria."

"You've got to be kidding! A food server?" The clerk snaps Crocker's change on the counter as if she prefers not to touch his fingers.

~

One hundred and fifty calories per pastry. Four grams of fat. Each gram of fat contains nine calories. The AMA and the surgeon general recommend lowering fat intake to twenty percent of daily calories. Thirty percent? Ten?

Both Ahmad and Pop now sit in the red convertible, watching their spicy breaths spout in the cold night air above their heads. Under the stall's fluorescent lights, their lips appear silvered, like blueberries. The silver on blueberries has its very own name. Go close enough to a subject and you will find—if its qualities receive sufficient handling— names.

Actually, Crocker *gave* these shivering boys the two sweaters he had received at Christmas. If either ever wore one, Crocker missed it. In their embrace of the hard sell, the boys prefer "muscle shirts," sleeveless, form-fitting things they wear on even the coldest days, and which leave them looking like the goosefleshed kids who hook old guys in the city.

"To imagine a language means to imagine a way of life." —*Ludwig Wittgenstein.* So reads the line of type that Crocker has taped to the top of the rickety desk of his school office.

"No, thanks," says Ahmad to Crocker's offer of coconut pastries. His eyes appear rheumy, as if he has been smoking dope, drinking. "No eat shit," Ahmad says.

Crocker barely manages to rock back on his heels, laugh. "So," he teases—playing the teacher/fool, a role he despises—"I suppose you boys finished your homework?"

Pop hoots with laughter. His eyes are eerie—a blue that appears milky against his dark skin. While Pop laughs, Ahmad looks away. He keeps his hands tucked hard in the pockets of his snaky jacket, as if this helps him to hold down his shivers.

"Come on next door," says Crocker. "I'll buy you coffee. You boys look chilly."

Pop looks to Ahmad. Who squints at a small tan car chugging out of the market lot and into the street. "Yes," says Ahmad, "yes, okay," and unfolds his handsome bones from behind the steering wheel, and opens the door.

Ahmad saunters. Ahmad hugs his elbows and doesn't talk. Ahmad's jaw stands out in a tight knob. While—in zigzags, smiling at the two of them, hooting—Pop runs backwards across the lot and toward the store.

Crocker thinks of himself young, running to outfox the cold. "See the full moon?" he calls ahead to Pop.

Gibbous. Very white. White rock. Matte as sponge when seen through a telescope. In Crocker's terrible dreams, the moon does not appear, Crocker is not a man at all. Crocker is an atom-size observer, set in place to receive cruel and unrelenting stimulation at the hands of the newly revealed universe. Where is the moon in Crocker's dreams? In his dreams, does he float, perhaps, beyond that side that we on earth never see?

(From the 1940s, an experiment: Subjects are asked to quickly identify a number of cards. One comes up marked with a number six and a red spade. The subjects identify this as a six of spades, or, sometimes, as a six of hearts. Shown the card again, however, for a longer period of time, they hesitate in their identifications; certain subjects declare themselves no longer certain they actually *recall* the shape of a spade.)

In an attempt at jocularity, Crocker tells the boys, "We always see the same face, you know; always the same side," and he pats his cheeks, and grins.

Obediently, the boys offer the moon a second, bored look; then they step through the convenience-market door.

"So." The clerk frowns while Crocker counts out his change for the coffees. She points at the pastries he has laid on the counter. "So are those the ones you bought before, or different?"

"The same. I thought my friends would like them—"

When Crocker turns to smile at the brothers, he finds Ahmad, lips drawn back like those on an angry dog. Ahmad is gesturing to Pop with some urgency, one hand holding the younger boy by the back of the neck.

"Look," says the clerk. She leans forward rakishly, one elbow on the counter. Crocker hopes the boys do not try to flirt with her. The boys seem to have acquired their sense of courtship from X-rated cable TV and clumsy work with dictionaries. "Beautiful girl," Crocker once heard Ahmad cry in the hallway, "come close to let me see the pudendum."

"What's the trouble?" says the clerk.

"I'm paying," says Crocker. "No trouble."

Ahmad nods. He picks up two of the steaming cups, takes a sip from one, and smiles at Crocker over the cup rim. "Hot," Ahmad says. He holds out the second cup to Crocker, and so it is that Crocker is extending his hand for the cup as the boy's elbows swing back—

Crocker cries out in pain and surprise as the coffee splashes his face—

"On legs!" yells Pop.

"On *knees!*" Ahmad says, an angry correction, and, with a swift crack from the almost comically dangerous-looking gun he whips from his jacket, he proceeds to create shattered lightning and rolls of thunder across the back of Crocker's skull.

A glowing moment.

Pink. Gold. Mentholated.

Crocker subtracts himself from it long enough to bid good-bye to his wife and son.

But finds himself alive. Still alive *now*. And alive *now*, too. Down on the floor. Everything above him is sun—terrible—and he blinks and considers his dear life, and how, maybe, maybe, they'll shoot the clerk first; and maybe that moment of concentrated attention might allow Crocker a scramble toward the banged-up metal doors leading to the storeroom—

"Tell girl, Crocker!" So shouts one of the robbers. Robbers, gunmen, assailants; personality vanquished in the battle with function. "Give key! We shoot!"

"Here!" the clerk sobs. "Here! Here!"

One boy presses a foot on Crocker's neck. Melting snow drips from a shoe onto Crocker's face, his hair.

If you had told Crocker, once upon a time, that he would someday be a customer in a convenience store during its robbery, he would have said, "I'm not surprised."

He is surprised.

When the robbers go—with a miraculous swish of doors, roar of car, ripped gravel—Crocker stays on his knees. He considers the melted snow—now warm on his skin—and his remarkable breath, the charming coils of his guts, the delivery of messages of injury that travel from his banged-up skull and coffee-scalded face to his brain, so nicely protected by a basically intact skull, which, like every other part of his body, presses against its delicate husk in grateful articulation.

A purple gum ball beneath the candy display beside Crocker's head. Grape. Next to the gum ball: a bit of fuzz. On the racks, Jolly Rancher candies flavored with cinnamon. Slo-Poke suckers. An open box of lucky rabbit's foot key chains. So people still buy lucky rabbit's feet. Crocker extends a finger to one of the feet, finds the tiny claws hidden in its fur.

Lucky.

"I can't believe this!" The clerk comes out from behind the counter to nudge Crocker with her foot. Rather hard. Actually, some might describe her movement as a kick. "Were you in on this?" she demands.

Crocker steadies himself with a hand on the counter, and gets slowly to his feet. "Was I in on it?" He smiles at the clerk, and gingerly touches the aching knob on the back of his head. "I guess I taught them how to use the imperative," he says.

Asks the clerk, "Is that the kind of gun they had?" From beneath the counter she brings out a box of pink tissues and hands it to Crocker. "If you weren't in on it, why did they come in with you?"

Crocker dabs at his wet collar and neck. Coffee, dirt, not blood. The wound to his head cannot be much, though the pain bellows impressively, on and off, like a foghorn or a smoke detector, some warning device designed to come in pulses so that the ear might not adjust, tune out the sound.

"They're my students," he says. "I don't know what they were thinking of."

The clerk shakes her head. She dials 911. She places her hand over the mouthpiece of the telephone and whispers, "Look." With a pointy elbow, she indicates a station wagon, now lumbering across the uneven parking lot. "Look, you'll have to help that customer while I'm talking to the cops."

Crocker nods. On the counter, steaming, the third—and last—cup of coffee still sits. Carefully, he takes it up in his hands. The Styrofoam is warm; the coffee, hot. It seems to him an elixir, more sacred than any communion wine drunk in his youth. A prophecy has been fulfilled, Crocker thinks, some sort of prophecy, and he takes a drink from the magic cup, and helps a hefty woman in house slippers to locate a bottle of maraschino cherries.

⌇

The police: one a woman, one a man wearing makeup apparently meant to give him a fierce, foreign air—sooty brows and lashes, a sticky orangish complexion. Just come from an underground operation, perhaps? A costume ball? Crocker smiles at both and does not mention the crack to his skull; nor does the clerk, who, in attending to her own pain, perhaps missed the blow entirely. "Really," says Crocker, "I have to be going. My wife and son." The officers smile. They drink coffee, and, with a tidy hand cupped under the chin to catch crumbs, eat the coconut pastries for which Crocker no longer has an appetite.

Crocker's step, crossing the parking lot, is springy; he does not mind if anyone smirks. A sweet, musty smell of hay fills his car: last summer's hay, hauled for mulch, now stirred up by the vacuum. And in his hair, beneath his fingers—now sensitive as a safecracker's—he finds grit. Grit from the melted snow that dripped from the boy's shoe, grit from this four-billion-some-year-old earth, or perhaps something older, something fallen out of the sky, cosmic dust picked up in our journey around the sun.

Crocker does not attempt to brush the grit away, but fingers the trails as he drives, as he goes up the silver-flecked walk to his shimmering house.

His wife. His wife will kiss the crack on his head. That is where the light shines in. His son—

"Surprise!" Many people stand in Crocker's little front hall. "Surprise! Happy birthday! You're late!" they say.

Toward the back of the crowd, his wife has a large plate of anger all cooked up, ready to serve, but this vanishes as guests at the front retreat in the face of Crocker's grimy injuries.

His wife cries out, "What happened?" and looks down in alarm at the blond child wiggling in her arms. Who notices nothing but his father's return. Wants only to be held.

Perhaps out of respect for the child, the guests ask their questions in light, almost gay voices. Perhaps for this reason, the guests quickly come to consider Crocker's experience nothing at all, an ill-fated movie everyone saw once upon a time, or heard discussed so often that even those who didn't see it feel as if they have, and now lay claim to its disregard. They drag Crocker to the living room and to its coffee table full of gifts: an inflatable alligator; a package of Pez candies in a dispenser topped by the head of Popeye the Sailor; a bottle of radiant blue nail polish; an impressively realistic puddle of rubber vomit. Everything has been selected specifically for its inappropriateness, its uselessness, its suggestion that Crocker needs nothing that can be purchased for under fifteen dollars.

Across the room, child in her lap, sits his wife, still pale from the scare, her pallor emphasized by the bright red scarf around her neck. There is a trick to the knot of the scarf. Standing in front of the bedroom mirror, the wife will loop the long red rectangle around her neck, then bring its ends together around and around her stiffened index finger, forming a kind of doughnut of silk that she pulls and fluffs and tweaks into a halo of soft folds. Crocker has watched his wife tie the scarf in this way many times, but never before realized she meant all of that tugging and plucking to add up to a rose.

"Excuse us," Crocker says, and lifts his son into his arms, takes his wife's pale hand, leads them both toward the kitchen. Looking back over her shoulder to the guests, his wife makes a funny face and points to a spot on her head that approximates the location of Crocker's bump. Loose screw, she mouths. She did want the evening to be a success, of course. Her own parody of bad taste sits in the little dining room: at each place at the table, a package of devil's food cakes coated in coconut and shaped like tiny igloos. Crocker spies this setup and, pleased, he laughs aloud.

"Here," he says when they reach the kitchen. He bundles his sports jacket around his son while his wife—with perfect understanding?—opens the door leading to the duplex's small wooden deck.

Out there, in the cold, they do not talk. After a time, the boy lays his head on Crocker's shoulder and closes his creamy eyelids and sleeps.

Crocker rests his own head atop his wife's. His wife's teeth chatter. Crocker feels the vibration as it passes through her skull, and he imagines her entire skeleton, the wide pelvis through which the boy descended, the stack of bones enclosing her spinal cord. And her circulatory system: think of her heart pumping, her hot and slippery liver purifying blood, the improbable wonder of this woman.

After a time, slowly, as if she imagines Crocker, too, might be asleep, his wife moves her head out from under his. "Do you know," she whispers, "if we lived on Neptune, the sun would hardly look brighter to us than any of these stars?"

Crocker nods, but he is distracted, listening to a sound in the distance, a car on the highway.

The boys, he thinks, and holds them on the road, directs them down the worst country gravel, and then over a river into which they throw the gun. Crocker makes the boys hopelessly lost. Then they run out of gas, abandon the red car, and—eyes open wide with fear—walk out into a snowy field under these very stars to a farmhouse that burns like a lantern in the distance.

A farm family is eating supper in the big yellow kitchen of the farmhouse. Mother, father, children, grandmother—all lift their heads at the knock.

The boys press their faces to the glass.

The startled farmer pushes back his chair. "What on earth?" he says as he opens the door; and the boys, too, use what language they have at that moment. They say, "Help us." No. They say, "Help us, please."

Home Ec

POLLY AND SUSAN have a baby. Who is the mother? Susan bore the baby, veins on her forehead gray as old sticks; but here is Polly, too, bamboo rake in hand, fluffing the apartment's sorry shag rug—flat as the coat on a piece of roadkill—here is Polly, one eye stuck like a burr to Nicko.

Nicko. Mr. Mouth. Playboy. Fuzzhead. That sweet mound on the couch, busily gnawing pink pillow welting. Mama, Nicko calls Polly. Mama, Nicko calls Susan.

Crackling blue eyes, hair white as taffy into which air, air, more and more air has been incorporated by tugs and twists and twists and pulls, Nicko scrambles from the couch, rear first, and tugs on the hem of Polly's shorts.

"You darling," Polly croons, and rests the bamboo rake against the apartment wall to give the boy a nuzzle. Polly is in a fine mood. Her raking aggravates Susan, true, but Polly finds it calming. When she rakes, Polly imagines herself, alternately, an old man with a pipe stuck in his back pocket, retired, happily at work on his yard; or a Zen monk, smoothing the sands of the monastery garden into swirls of infinite patience, mystical whirligigs.

Across the room, feet up on a hassock, the rest of her on the apartment's odious carpet: Susan. In the televised background, a knife gallops across a wooden chopping block as one more great chef from New Orleans demonstrates jambalaya.

Rice.

Polly wonders if it is possible that the sizzle of rice the chef pours into the pot could come from Susan's father's plantation.

Really: a *plantation*.

Here, in barren Arizona, when Susan says "plantation," Polly is sorry to say so, but Susan sounds a little snobby, even corrupt, as if she maybe grew up bossing around black mammies. According to Susan, however—in Susan's own book—"plantation" sounds far less exotic than "ranch."

Polly hails from the Midwest. Polly once asked Susan, "But couldn't you say 'farm'? Couldn't a farm be whatever you like?" To which Susan replied, cocking an eyebrow like a cartoon crow, an owl, a fox, any wise and sharp-tongued creature—always dramatic Susan, always thrilling—"Farm might be whatever *you* like, Pol, but it wouldn't be what a plantation is, which *is* a plantation!"

And just look at Susan over there in her red and gold brocade vest, her honey pageboy. Susan is a lovely jack of hearts—totally absorbed in the show's onion chopping—who every now and then takes a sip of chianti from what used to be a twenty-four-ounce jar of chunky peanut butter (the latest manifestation of Susan's resolve to drink but one drink a day). Polly has already asked what appeared on Susan's chalkboard menu at Chez Mes Amis today: bouillabaisse. Reportedly admired by all. Pot de cremes. A spicy dish from the Caribbean, hot with garlic and a red pepper special-ordered from Miami. People of all stripes love to eat at Chez Mes Amis. In its bright and cramped quarters, some feel as if they dine in their own kitchen, others as if they embark on a bold adventure. Polly—who financed the operation out of savings from a former life as a teacher of high school home ec—Polly falls into the latter group.

"Rrrh," says Susan. Susan lets her tongue hang from her mouth like a beat dog's. With the tip of her nose, Polly finds Nicko's pink shell of ear fuzzy as a caterpillar, intoxicating, wonderful.

"Let's order pizza," says Susan. "I asked Martina Hassapopolous to come by and I ain't about to cook one more iota!"

Polly smiles as if amused by the bouncing name—its echo, its burden of olive eyes and dark hair as dense as ash in a grate—but happiness sifts right out of Polly these days, a sly leakage now so familiar Polly has come to visualize the loss in terms of a war movie she saw long, long ago, and the dirt the movie's tunneling war prisoners discreetly scattered from bags inside their pant legs while crossing the prison compound.

Susan does not love Polly anymore. Polly does not talk to Susan about this development; perhaps Susan does not yet *know* she no longer loves Polly, and Polly should not bring the fact to her attention. They are a family now, after all; they must protect more than their passion these days.

"But, Susan," says Polly. Being provocative, she knows. Sometimes she cannot help being provocative. "We don't *like* pizza, Susan."

"*Martina* likes pizza," says Susan, and, as she is wont to do during irritable moments, dips farther down South to heighten all effects: "*Martina* is our guest, child. And will you please please *please* try to look like *somethin'* when she comes on by?"

Polly grins and wipes her hands over her cropped head. Secretly, she is tunneling, shoring up walls, working without appearing to work.

And where will Polly's secret tunnel come out? Nowhere. It will be a cozy thing, a rabbit warren, an endless maze.

"Susan," she says, and looks up from tying Nicko's shoe in a wad of double knot, "did you notice this bump on Nicky's neck?"

"That thing? That's nothing, child. That's hemangioma."

Hemangioma. Hemangioma, carcinoma. Susan handles the word as if it's ordinary as "apple," "Scotch tape," "napkin." Polly is certainly a better mother than Susan. Polly would die for Nicko. She has imagined it many times, rehearsed the necessary bravery so there can be no question of backing down.

"He could be susceptible," says Polly. "We really don't know." She blows a star in the boy's pale hair. "I read where there's mice that carry a gene—ninety percent of them actually d-i-e if they get exposed to bells or jangling keys in excess of two minutes."

"In *excess* of two minutes? Jangling *keys?*" Susan sits up, laughing. Her fine posture—acquired during a brief and overheated apprenticeship in the Brouhaha Theater of Portland, Oregon—affects Polly like the scary and exciting tornado warnings strung across TV screens of her youth. Polly holds her breath.

"Well," says Susan, "he don't look like mice to me, honey." And lies back on the floor and stares at the apartment's popcorn ceiling. "But, of course, feeblemindedness, manic depression, schizophrenia, criminality . . . all *do* have their genetic component."

Out of loyalty to her sad and loony mom, Polly does a little mental conjuring of Susan's absolutely bourbon-soaked parents. Polly imagines saying to Susan, "Alcoholism, too, Susan. Alcoholism may be genetic." She does not say this, however, because she does not, in any way, want to cast a shadow on sweet Nicko's future. Instead, she says, "Just remember, Susan, when my mom comes to visit, she *can't* eat pizza."

"Lord god almighty!" Susan pummels the hassock with her heels. Clouds of dust—dust that enters the apartment all year round, traveling over the complex's drip-irrigated greenery as if scenting out its true home—clouds of dust rise in the late afternoon sunshine. "Your mother ain't even here!" says Susan.

"But when she visits—"

"When your folks come, Polly, we'll give them one of them doohickeys like at the hospital," says Susan, and draws a box in the air with her index finger. "'Check one from each category: Cooked carrots or green beans. Filet of fish or baked chicken. Orange gelatin or the butterscotch pudding.'"

Even now, Polly cannot help but think, *That menu could use a leafy vegetable.*

"Only soft foods for the maniacal mom!" cries Susan. She leaps onto the couch and, one foot on the armrest, strikes a pirate's pose. "No sharp objects! Give the woman a runcible spoon!"

Polly blinks, an appearance of bafflement her latest resource; in fact, Polly knows "runcible spoon" from Nicko's *The Owl and the Pussycat*. And her own childhood's book. Read to her by her own mom, so long ago, in a voice that dipped up and down and carried Polly in its own friendly boat. Light travelers, the Owl and the Pussycat took with them a runcible spoon, useful for dining upon both mince and slices of quince.

"She's not a maniac," Polly says hopefully, but Susan does not stick around to retract terminology. "Hi-yah!" she cries, and bounds down the hall to take one of her inimitably long showers.

Why couldn't Polly take a shower for as long as Susan?

She carries Nicko over to the sliding glass door. The wonderful boy winds his arms around her neck. "Uh," he says, and points intelligently to a mockingbird perched on a clipped block of pyracantha.

"Is that your song, little bird?" Polly says through the screen. "Do you know the difference?" The bird sings wildly. Polly tries to re-create the notes for Nicko while Nicko watches a family splash in the complex's bright blue swimming pool. The father of the family tosses the children high into the air, and they scream in terror and delight. Nicko yawns sweetly. Dream boy, celestial cupcake. Polly draws her chin back and forth over the top of his silken head.

First Polly wanted a baby, and Susan—hoping to perform at A.K.A. Theater—did not. Then, after a particularly quarrelsome visit from Susan's parents, Susan wanted a baby, also. Who would have the baby? They were still happy together back then, Polly and Susan. The question kept them up late, Susan drinking Wild Turkey, smoking and every now and then making a wonderful grab across the kitchen table for Polly's hand.

Who would be the father?

Polly imagined all decisions floated before them like happy holidays. A mistake. One fine day, she entered the kitchen, and there stood

Susan, grinning, stabbing a table knife into a can of frozen orange juice.

"What's up?" Polly asked.

"Oh!" sang Susan. She pressed her hands to her face, covering her grin. She kicked her feet from side to side, banging the cupboard doors. Polly giggled, but felt a little scared. "What is it?" she asked.

Susan looked out from over the tips of her fingers, as if she contained uncontrollable delight: "I'm pregnant!"

Polly's first impulse was to choke her.

(1) How could Susan be pregnant?

(2) Didn't she, Polly, want to have the baby?

Susan pressed her forehead to Polly's forehead; intimate, yes, but difficult to look into Susan's eyes from this position. "I realized, genetically speaking," said Susan, "that I was, you know, the one who ought to chance it, but I didn't tell you in case things didn't . . . take."

"'Things'?" said Polly.

The frozen concentrate made a sucking sound as Susan drew the fat orange plug forth on the knife. "The sperm, Polly! From the sperm bank! Aren't you happy? If you're not happy, I'll just blow my brains out right this minute!"

"Of course I'm happy," Polly said. Her fingers grabbed at the insides of her sweater pockets. Where are the bills? she wanted to ask. Who was the doctor? A parade of privately owned penises blurred her vision, formed a throbbing tangle of suspicion behind her left eye.

"I just can't believe it!" she said, which covered a lot of territory. Polly always made sure she said what needed to be said in such a way that at least *she* could hear her own indictments.

~

Martina Hassapopolous is twenty-seven, six years younger than Susan, eight years younger than Polly. Her skin fits gold and tight.

A laughing Susan tells serious Polly—Nicko on her hip, bent over the boy's dresser in search of a navy sock—that last week this Martina offered Susan a muscle-bound stereo salesman, *but today, honey, today took all. Today it was her hairdresser, straight but very fem. This is Martina's idea of how I might get weaned off liking women, you see?*

Polly nods and offers a representation of the mildest possible amusement. Martina Hassapopolous speaks in a husky stage whisper. Initially, Susan did hilarious imitations of Martina's vamping: no more. Martina Hassapopolous has a widow's peak and—like a number of very attractive people Polly has met—passionately delivered but loosely held opinions. The day Polly met her, at work at Chez Mes Amis, Martina shouted at Polly, "Listen, you're going to make that kid crazy if you don't quit carting him around so much!" For emphasis, Martina scraped Susan's prized boning knife *right* along the kitchen's brick wall. Polly waited for Susan to yell. Susan did not yell. Susan offered Martina a glass of white wine and told her to put her feet up, rest, just relax, please.

And now here comes Martina—a bit furry, but definitely sexy—following two out-thrust bottles of something alcoholic right into Susan and Polly's apartment and saying, "Driving in that suicide lane at six-fifteen! Never again! Okay! Drink up! No slackers!"

Susan, hair still wet from the shower, walks into the room on her hands, just as she did during her role for *Harlequin, Yes!* You would think, looking at grinning Sue, that nothing in the world pleased her so much as bossy intensity. She rights herself, but stays on her knees in front of Martina. "Give me one of those bottles, you brilliant child!" she cries. "Polly here ain't a drinker since Nick came along, and I must warn you, she won't be much of a hostess either once the telephone rings. Her mama and daddy can't get by one single day without knowing how their darling fares."

"Nice to see you, Martina," says Polly. She can scarcely hear her own voice over the duel of manners and self-preservation in her head; and by the time she offers Martina a seat, Martina has her feet tucked up under her skirt, and owns over one half of the couch. Susan dances in front of Martina, and laughs and says, "Honey, did I ever tell you about the first time Pol's parents came for a visit, and Pol's mom went

into what Pol and her daddy called a 'spell'?" Susan winks at Polly, as
if Polly herself arranged the details of that nightmare for best enter-
tainment value. "A spell! Honey, the woman put one entire box of
Cream of Wheat cereal into the pressure cooker while the rest of us sat
watching a little girl ice skater on the television set! Cream of Wheat!
On high! Cream of Wheat all over the ceiling! We came a-running at
the noise—boom, and then plop, plop, plop!" Susan splays her fingers
on her cheeks and opens her eyes in comic horror. She drops her head
back as far as it will go and draws extravagant breaths through her
nose. "*She*—the perpetrator—we found lying beneath the bedroom
drapes, which for reasons unknown she had yanked from their rods!"

"Oh, stop!" says Martina. A pretty laugher.

Susan collapses beside her on the couch. "Uproar is the woman's
game," Susan declares. "She made poor Pol here into a wreck, then
said things like: 'Why, Polly, I was just whipping us up a snack!' and 'If
somebody'd hung those drapes right in the first place, dear, they
wouldn't have come down so easy!'"

Martina emits another lovely whoop of laughter. Any moment
now, the phone will ring, offer Polly some relief. Susan catches Polly
looking at her watch, and she cries, "Is it a liftoff, Polly? Ten! Nine!
Eight! Seven! Six—"

The phone rings.

～

In the kitchen, Polly listens to her father's cheerful recital of supper.
Now and then, she peeks out at Nicko, cruising happily around the
coffee table to whose four sharp corners Polly has affixed sturdy foam
bumpers. Martina and Susan eat pizza, fangs of mozzarella and tomato
sauce stretched perilously over the carpet and couch.

Polly's parents consider Polly a good Christian soul to live with an
unmarried mother. "How's that little Nicholas?" Polly's father asks.

For the moment, safe, examining an unbreakable ashtray.

But Martina's arm lies across the back of the couch, almost touching Susan's shoulder. Polly tries not to fret. With this Martina, it must just be vanity, curiosity. Martina merely wants to see herself reflected on some little lake in Susan and Polly's particular landscape. So Polly forces herself to look away. In order to make good use of her time on the phone, she soaks paper towels with white vinegar and lays them on the lime deposits ringing the spigot and the faucet handles.

Polly's mother has been having a hard time lately. When she comes on the line, she makes a high, yawning sound, like ice heaving on the creeks of Polly's childhood. Polly's father takes the phone back quickly. "Mom's still under the weather, aren't you, honey?" he says, and then, to Polly, "How's that article coming?"

Polly tries to remember: Coin-operated laundries? Tanning beds in beauty salons? Polly's parents believe Polly supports herself these days by writing freelance articles for trade magazines: *Food Service News. World of Spas.* "Not anything you'd ever see on the newsstand," she told them. "Heck, I never see 'em myself! They just disappear into the corporate maw!" Susan had made Polly a gift of "the corporate maw." "The corporate maw?" her parents said, so far always inclined to laugh in proud delight when they did not understand what their dear Polly meant.

~

The apartment feels all wrong when Polly gets off the phone, and no wonder: the living room, the bedroom, the bath—all stand empty.

She opens the sliding door. In the swimming pool—unattended—the two children she saw earlier take turns diving off the steps into the shallow end, and Polly shouts to them, "Where are your parents? Get out of that water this instant!" Frightened, the children scramble from the water and run away, crying, "Mom! Dad!"

Polly does not know what sort of car Martina drives but it is certain that Polly and Susan's car no longer sits in the parking lot.

"I bet she didn't even take the safety seat!" Polly exclaims aloud, and rushes back to the apartment to check. Sure enough, there is the seat!

In the kitchen, she dials the telephone number of Sam and Katherine, fellow teachers from her days at Catalina High. Sam and Katherine will help her. They will make her feel deserving of sympathy. It was Sam and Katherine who helped Polly explain things to Susan the time that—feeling neglected by Susan—Polly mailed herself a series of obscene and very scary unsigned letters. They are nice people, Sam and Katherine. Normal. Married.

After a time of listening to the telephone ring at Sam and Katherine's house, Polly remembers something awful: Sam and Katherine are in San Diego, herding their children through Sea World. They will not return for two days, an amount of time that strikes Polly as unbearable.

She lays her cheek on the kitchen counter. She imagines Nicko rolling about in the back of the Datsun.

At Chez Mes Amis, there is a recording. To Polly's surprise, on the recording, her own sturdy Midwestern voice has been supplanted by Martina's borderless purr: "You'll find us open from ten A.M. to four P.M. Monday through Saturday, serving a limited but visionary menu."

"I know you're there, Susan," says Polly, "and I want you to bring Nicko home. This is serious. You've been drinking."

Polly feels as if she speaks into outer space. Do you read me? Come in.

"Hey, Polly," says Susan.

Polly takes a breath. "What are you doing, Susan?"

"We came down for some more wine, child."

More wine. Nicko's college education running down their throats and out their bladders and into the restaurant's stylish black toilet. Yet Susan is having fun! Listen! Nicko is in the background, laughing at a song sung by the terrible Martina.

"When are you coming home, Susan?"

"Home?"

"Susan," says Polly, the air around her suddenly polar, glossy with panic. "Bring Nicko home, please."

"After a while," says Susan. She sounds as if she stands by a window in a cabin, as if she discusses the condition of the lake before her.

"What's Nicky doing, Susan?"

"Oh, he's having a grand time, Pol, drinking a Shirley Temple and being entertained by Martina."

"Susan," says Polly, "if you don't bring him home right now, I'm not kidding, I'm going to kill myself."

Susan does not respond for a moment; then she laughs. "I'm sure I didn't hear you correct," she says. "I'm sure you wouldn't dream of threatening me."

"The gas is on," says Polly. How odd. How awful. And for what? All four burners hiss, plus the oven, the odor like something rancid. Does this mean she is nuts, or just an idiot? They will never give her Nicko now. Not that they would have anyway.

Susan sighs like a troubled employer. "I'm calling Kath and Sam," she says. "I'll let them in on your little scene. How do you like them apples?"

Polly explains about Sea World, San Diego.

"Damn it, Polly!"

"Are you coming home?"

"Turn off that gas!"

"Are you coming home?"

"I'm calling the police is what *I'm* doing," says Susan.

~

Polly draws the curtains. Turns off the lights. Sits in a rocker that once belonged to her grandmother. Outside, cars turn in and out of the parking lot. Someone dives into the pool with a splash and a laugh. Polly pretends not to care about the age of the swimmer, the condition. She rocks. In her heart of hearts, she suspects she will never be able to move into that world—exquisite, if terrible—that her mother can sometimes hole up in for weeks at a time. All Polly has is this pale imitation of something outward: the curtains drawn, the rocking.

She used to find her mother that way, after walking home from grade school. Her mother seemed like a mythical creature then, the queen frog in her green forest; she might smile at Polly, but she did not wish to be disturbed.

A siren sings in the distance, comes closer. Polly's heart beats hard. Doors open and close. Feet pound in the hallway, and there is knocking. "Open up, Miss Threlkeld, or we'll break down the door!"

The door will be expensive to repair, Polly supposes, but how stirring to hear them batter at it. Blam, blam, she feels the percussion in her chest. For a while, it seems the thing will never give way, but then it swings—crack—against the wall, and there in the lighted hallway stand two police officers and a few neighbors. These neighbors never have become friends of Polly's, and after the officers step inside—one heading for Polly, one for the kitchen—the neighbors stay by the doorway. So wary. Actually frightened, it seems. As if they already know Polly as a creature made unreliable by long years in captivity, and so she does her best to smile their way, to show them all she really means no harm.

Blood and Gore

I LIVE ON RADIAL Highway so the place I usually go is up Blondo to Fifty-sixth. I'm only telling you since there's room for more. I go up Blondo, then left on Fifty-sixth so I end up looking down on Happy Hollow Boulevard. That's Mondays and Saturdays. There, I got the advantage of being up on a rise, plus the corner lots. A buddy told me the big bushes people in that neighborhood put in can run a thousand bucks apiece. On my corner, though, the old lady keeps her yard slick as a mole's back, and the yard across the way's not half bad, either. If anything comes down the boulevard, I see it early, I hop right on it. Also, somebody's always working on the grass and trees up there. Chemlawn—you've probably seen their trucks—but lots use guys out of pickups, which means nobody never notices me.

Say, it's nice there! All the fancy brick. Hardly nobody comes out or goes in, which makes it almost like being in the country, except cleaner and with sidewalks. Once, just after Halloween, I seen a squirrel sitting on the old lady's lawn, eating a miniature Milky Way bar! Right in its hands! That was the cutest darned thing! If I'd had a camera on me, I could have won a prize in the Sunday supplement, what do you bet?

The old lady has a humpback. I seen her when she put on a garage sale last fall. There were some real lookers poking around in the stuff there, so I got out of my truck and went up, too. One I got next to, I asked what did she think about some Christmas lights they had there. Did she think they'd work right? That sort of thing. If you stood just so, she had on a big shirt, and you could see between the buttons. *She* didn't know! She went on talking to me, fishing around in a box of kitchen things. "So," I says, "you live around here or what? You live in one of these houses?" *That* spooked her. Off she sneaked, over to the card table where the humpback and her friends were taking the money. All them looked at me real quick, then pretended they hadn't. That was the day I picked up my power drill. Black & Decker. Runs like new. I was set to pay for it—it even has the bits that come with it—but when I got near the pay table, the ladies just looked away, like they wanted me to pass on by. What the hell, I figured, and I took the drill out to the truck. Five bucks was all the old lady wanted for the drill. That's not much.

The garage sale would have been back when I got off Saturdays. Everybody at work who didn't have Saturdays *wanted* Saturdays, they *had* to have Saturdays so they could haul their boats to the lake. All them boo-hooed, Saturday, Saturday. I never could see anything so hot about Saturday. I couldn't sleep in Saturdays with the cartoons playing, and if I got up to watch, a pack of kids sat on me, a lot of peed pants ruining the start of a day their mother was going to turn to pure hell, anyway, with talk of chores and so on. Finally, over break one day, I says—casual, since I mostly keep clear of them at work—"If there's trouble for the other fellows, you know, I could take Mondays instead."

Let me tell you, they about spilled their thermoses. Then, real quick, all them settled back like they hardly heard what I said. "That's real decent of you, Eule," they said. "Maybe one of us can make the switch." Shit for brains is what they got, while I got *me* a quiet house Mondays, and Saturdays I sneak out while the rest sleep, and I look around a little before work.

Women in my neighborhood don't run, which is just as well considering the rear ends on most. If all them started to run, they'd bust up the concrete. Also true for the wife. She got the idea I should be in with her when the last one was born. Blood and gore. *That* put me off sex, believe me. That's birth control number one.

But what I started to tell: Last Saturday, I went out to look around before work, and something happened a little different. I went down the hill for the first gal okay. I had things timed so I got to the corner just about the time she did. I stopped a little into the crosswalk so she'd have to go around me. This one was hefty, and when she come around the front of the truck, I said, real slow, "Hip-po." She got all red in the face, which gave me a laugh. Then I drove on past her, down Happy Hollow. I waved to her, like I'd just happened to be passing through. I always do that.

Then I drove back to Blondo and around again. When I got to my lookout, though, the old lady's yardman had parked his truck wrong and screwed up my view! I *almost* missed what came down the street next, which is what I was going to tell you about. This one was a college girl. University T-shirt and shorts, fancy running shoes. Ponytail. Just in time I rolled down to the stop, and I called to her:

"Say there!"

She acted a little spooked, but not so bad as the first. This one knew she was cute. I tooted at her when I drove past. She kept looking straight ahead, real snotty.

After I got parked again, some kids come by carrying fishing poles. Where do you suppose they catch fish around Happy Hollow? I get bullheads out by Boystown, but I think those boys were dreaming if they meant to catch fish in the creek there. I drank a cup of coffee from my thermos and smoked a cigarette. I guess I fell asleep for a while. I don't remember doing that on a Saturday since I took Mondays. I don't have to start work 'til eight, but still, I was pushing my luck that time.

Anyway, I looked up, and here come the college girl again, this time going the opposite direction, only now all pink and sweaty and tuckered out. To give her a start, I didn't turn my engine on, I just rolled down toward the stop. That truck can whisper when I want it to. The girl didn't even see me 'til I was in the crosswalk, and then instead of stopping or going behind me, like a fool she darted out into Happy Hollow.

Kaboom!

Up she went on the hood of this car going by, off she bounced. Blood and gore.

I set my parking brake and got out.

It was a guy in a yellow Trans Am that hit her—one of those cars that was a real beauty maybe ten years ago but now it's all rusted to hell. You know what I mean. Nobody had taken care of that car at all. People who won't take care of a car like that don't even deserve to own it. A car like that—during winter, when they salt—you got to clean off the undercarriage every time. You don't clean the undercarriage every time, there's your investment, poof.

Anyway, this guy from the Trans Am kneeled down by the mess he'd made of that girl. Her eyes were open but she wasn't going to be seeing nothing no more, if you know what I mean. Still, the guy goes, "Somebody call an ambulance!" He grabs at his shirt like he means to get in a fight with himself. "Somebody call an ambulance!"

Of course, except for the yardmen, people in that kind of neighborhood were mostly still to bed. An older guy was out walking his dogs, and these dogs—they were big dogs, a Doberman and a shepherd—they could smell that meat in the road. It was really something, believe me. It was all that old guy could do to keep the dogs back, and he was shouting at them, and kicking, and then the old lady with the hump come hobbling out.

"Oh, my lord!" she goes. "I'll call! I'll call!" You should have seen her run! She wore this fancy pink bathrobe, all hiked up funny because of the hump!

The guy from the Trans Am sat there in the road, patting at the girl's head. Well. Jesus. I mean, part of it's over on the curb, if you catch my drift, and he's saying, "You ran right out in front of me! Didn't you see me?"

I went up a little closer. I don't like to get involved but I tapped the guy on the shoulder. "Hey," I said, "don't sweat, buddy. You got a witness, okay? I'm here. I seen it, okay?"

I was in the paper because of that. Not my name, but they talked about the witness, and that was me. The guy in the Trans Am didn't get charged with nothing and I was the one that saved his neck. Just by being in the right place at the right time, I was the one that could step forward and set things to right, just by saying "I was there and this is what happened."

Voodoo Girls on Ice

IT HAD BEEN snowing for days. The window seat in the Pierce kitchen held an evening paper all lit up with color photos testifying to the storm's extravagance: a trio of people in fluorescent caps skied off the roof of a barn and down onto the lake; a woman dug a lavender tunnel in the direction of her greenhouse; and there were cars, too, buried, their barely exposed rooftops bright and tempting as shells on a sandy beach.

Heather Pierce and I sat in the kitchen—her parents' kitchen, I would say now, but back then it was still Heather's kitchen, too—a handsome, cozy room, cram-packed with early American reproductions.

Heather and I drank vodka. To soften its blows, we kept our mouths full of lemon drops. Before discovering vodka with lemon drops, Heather and I had tried vodka mixed with Tab. Diet Rite Cola. Orange juice. Chocolate milk. Fresca. Grape soda. We were sixteen years old. Best friends, but on the skids.

"*Shards* of bone," Heather said. "*Barbed* wire." She was uncharacteristically energetic that night. Ever since I'd arrived at the house, she had been snapping her teeth, tossing her head around like a Doberman. She rose out of her chair to bring her face close to mine as she detailed how, the night before, a boy from our school—someone by the name of Kevin Hammersmith—this Kevin had lost control of his car on a country road, spun out across a cornfield at a high rate of speed. Heather frowned, tipped her forehead toward me. I couldn't see her eyes when she slashed her fingers across her neck, made a slippery, gurgling noise to indicate how a string of barbed wire had decapitated the boy; still, I took her gesture as meant for me in more ways than one—something threatening that had to do with my neglect of her over the last year.

I tried to deflect all that by acting weary, a little bored with her story. "Jesus, Heather," I said, "that's enough."

She looked up at me, then: "So you *were* listening!"

"Of course I was listening." I looked away and toward the dark dining room, the street beyond. Outside, big snow plows roared past the house, and their revolving lights made terrible passes through the window; the lights blanched the dining room chairs, made the chairs pulse with ghostly energy—any moment now, it seemed those chairs might push themselves away from the empty table, crash on through the windowpanes in pursuit of the beams that had brought them to life.

"*Merde!*" Heather cried, then grinned when I turned to her. I grinned back. Heather used to ask me to set up dates for her and I tried. The boys always objected that she was too tall, but they were idiots and they'd know it a few years down the road. Heather was lovely, with full lips and the sort of chocolate eyes that made all other colors seem faded, overexposed. Still, that night, drunk on vodka, she looked odd, her skin glassy and red and, worse, that morning, she'd dyed her caramel-colored hair to a black so strawy and bunched up on either side of the part she might as well have dropped an open dictionary on her head.

"All right." She pressed the backs of her hands to her cheeks, the way some people do when checking their temperatures. "Listen," she said, "something incredible has happened, Jenny." She hurried to the base of the stairs leading to the second floor. Listening for her parents.

We were always on guard against our parents' catching us at one thing or another: Heather, because hers thought well of her; I, because mine had a tendency to hit, push, throw whatever wasn't nailed down.

Heather and I had been friends since we were nine years old and signed up for the same swim class at the YWCA. Together, we'd listened to our older siblings' recordings of the Stones and her dad's *Madama Butterfly* and *Turandot*. In each other, we'd found our ideal playmate. Heather not only liked books but she knew as well as I that when our Barbie dolls fell asleep on a picnic, our Ken dolls should take advantage of the opportunity to remove the Barbies' cute outfits and press up against their naked bodies. Together, Heather and I had prepared for romance the way some people prepare for careers as ballerinas or concert pianists. In the spring of eighth grade, in my eagerness to show Heather the Emily Dickinson poem "I cannot live with you," I ran all of the way across town from my own junior high school so I might be at Heather's own school when it let out. And how had I felt that day, legs scissoring through the spring air? Joyful to be going to my friend.

Two years later, however, sitting in the Pierces' kitchen, watching Heather stand at the base of the stairs to listen for her parents, I knew things had changed. I had fallen in love with a boy from the local college and been neglectful of Heather. While love had me pinned to the backseat of an ancient Chevrolet, Heather acquired new friends. More and more often, I felt dispossessed in her company—like one of those old lords who had stayed away from the kingdom too long and, upon returning, found his castle gone, the stones carted off to become the walls of other people's houses, or pens for confining hogs and cattle.

Still, when Heather said, "We're safe," and, smiling, turned away from the stairs, I felt at home. I knew where I sat: in a ladder-back chair I'd sat in hundreds of times. I knew the source of the little shadow that hung like a broken thumb on the kitchen's far wall: Mrs. Pierce's antique butter mold, single-serving, thistle design carved in its bottom. I knew where Mrs. Pierce kept her string and Elmer's glue, and that paper bags for lining the trash basket sat at the back of the bread drawer.

Boys, I want to say now. *Boys.* As if they explain everything, and of course they don't. But they *did* lurk behind most of our problems, didn't they? *Boys,* after all, were the silver on the mirror that gave us back our reflections, or didn't, and so, naturally, Heather and I thought boys were the most important things in the world.

Heather did a little dance that night as she came back across the kitchen toward me. "What it is," she said, "I don't want my parents to hear, but I've found out I'm a *witch,* Jenny! Kevin Hammersmith was a techie for the play and *I* put a curse on him at the cast party. I'm the one who made him die!"

She stared hard at me. I don't know what she expected, but while she took a chair at the table, I squeezed one eye shut and, with the other, stared across the silver ring of refractions caught on the vodka bottle's lip. A witch: this struck me as not so much impossible as untenable. Yes, I had come prepared to jump through a few hoops to get back in Heather's good graces, but I didn't mean to offer obeisance, and it would have taken obeisance for me to agree to her being a witch. This being the case, I tried to put some sort of woozy amusement on my face. God knows what I came up with. The boy with the Chevrolet recently had broken my heart, and I'd hardly slept since the occasion, hardly eaten. My thoughts had acquired a queer way of tumbling forward, an almost visual sensation, something like watching a defective television.

"Well, a *witch,*" I said.

Heather stood, spread her blunt fingers on the table, pressed down on their tips for balance. "Somebody brought a Ouija board to the party, and I couldn't make a mistake, Jen. I felt my power, head to toe!" She swept her arm through the air in a broad gesture characteristic of the attorney she'd recently portrayed in the school play. "Everyone there said I was a witch, but Kevin Hammersmith laughed, and that's when I put a curse on him."

Perhaps, I thought—bored, blue—perhaps I could bring the conversation around to my broken heart by edging us onto the subject of telepathy. I could explain how, each night, I lay in my bed and sent messages to the little college that sat above the lake, to the dormitory housing the boy who had broken my heart, and how I pictured those messages traveling along a beam of light—

"So?" Heather said. "Do you believe I'm a witch, Jenny?"

"Sure, why not?" I answered without enthusiasm.

In our reflections on the night-backed window, both of us sat with heads canted to one side, hands supporting cheeks. A dreamy, passive look favored by certain girls and women for studio portraits, though I couldn't have imagined a girl who didn't privately understand such postures expressed a nature gone underground, constant attendance to the construction of an effect.

The alcohol, of course, had competing claims. The alcohol had pushed both Heather and me a little faster to the point in the evening where we'd always begin to lose our fashionable gloss. Somewhere along the line, Heather already had smeared one eye's makeup; and I, through thoughtless leaning, had flattened half of my carefully arranged hair.

Beyond our reflections, the Pierces' yard looked strange, all the well-known bushes and fences canceled by the moonlit snow that swept down to the lake and on to the other side, where only the dark rim of trees suggested the shore.

"Jenny," Heather said, "I want you to drive me out there, to that cornfield where Kevin Hammersmith crashed."

I stared out the window, sucked on my boozy mouthful of lemon drops. At first, the drops always felt rough and dusty, like the cut edge of a piece of glass, but then they went silky smooth, yielded the very best song: Sweet! Sour! Sweet!

What was I willing to do to win back Heather's friendship? What was not too much? I rebelled at the idea of driving her to the accident site, standing out in some cold cornfield as if I believed Heather were fate's own engineer.

"Heather," I said, "I'm too drunk to drive."

She laughed. "When were you ever too drunk to drive, Jenny?"

At the time, I was young enough to feel flattered by this question, and warmed, too, by the way it pointed up the duration of our friendship. Heather knew me. Knew that I sometimes ended up in a ditch or ran over things that punched holes in gas tanks and screwed-up undercarriages, but that none of that ever stopped me from putting keys in ignitions and making my drunken way down whatever road lay before me.

"Okay," I said, "okay, I'll drive, but, Heather, you know, maybe it was just a *regular* accident."

She shook her head, hard. From her back pants' pocket, she brought out a curl of newsprint. "Look. We were just leaving the party when I put the curse on, and twenty minutes later, he's dead! Twelve *seventeen*."

I read the article through, though I'd read it that morning. Did I mean to seem interested now? Or to pretend the news hadn't even caught my eye earlier in the day? Both, and even the recognition of such contradictions seems inadequate.

According to the article, there had been a passenger in the Hammersmith car, John Arthur Gibbs, who had worn a seat belt and "suffered mild frostbite to the ears while walking to a nearby farm for assistance."

"Poor Gibbs," I said. "I suppose he wishes he'd lost at least a toe or something."

Heather tapped a finger on the accompanying photo. "Recognize Kevin?"

An invulnerable-looking boy, forehead a great white knee pressing out from behind a swag of dark, slippery bangs. Out of respect for the dead I stopped myself from pointing out his clear resemblance to the young Adolf Hitler.

"Can't say he rings a bell, Heather."

With great purpose and caution—they might have been the twin lids atop of steaming twin pots—Heather lifted her eyebrows. "I suppose you don't know who Tim Hungerford is either?" she said. "I cursed Tim Hungerford and he broke his arm."

During our freshman year, Heather had had a terrible crush on Tim Hungerford—Airedale hair, handsome Roman nose. Of course I knew who he was. In the school library, just days before, I had watched one of Tim's friends draw breasts upon a cast on Tim's arm; I had even witnessed the way in which the friend transformed the breasts into long-lashed eyes at the approach of the school librarian.

What did Heather want? To highlight my isolation? For me to pretend that I did not remember how humiliated she had felt over her failure with that boy?

"Hungerford?" I repeated the name as if it were so unfamiliar that I had a hard time fitting it into my mouth. What a relief, then, to hear Mr. and Mrs. Pierce on the stairs, to hiss, "Vodka, Heather," and hop off the window seat so she could set the bottle inside with the *National Geographic*s and road maps.

Heather's parents were sturdy, kind-hearted Midwesterners. In their party clothes, they looked vulnerable as little kids. "Hey," I said, "you guys are pretty snazzy tonight!"

"Why, thank you, Jenny!" Mr. Pierce wiggled his eyebrows around—lively wiggles, like something caught on a hook. He was always doing this, as if people amused and confounded him, which I suppose makes good sense.

I hardly admitted it to myself at the time, but I thought Heather was incredibly lucky to have such parents: Mr. Pierce, who actually asked Heather and me questions at dinner; Mrs. Pierce, with her sunny approval for Heather and my plans, our clothes, the little skits we used to make up and perform in the living room. Of course, now that I'd neglected Heather, things were different. Instead of smiles, Mrs. Pierce turned something like a searchlight on me. She treated me, I suppose, the way my mother had always treated Heather.

"You think that Heather's such a good friend of yours," my mother would say after Heather's visits, and then she'd explain how, oh, maybe, how while I was taking a shower, she'd overheard Heather *sniggering* on the phone, yes, and my mother was pretty darn sure that sniggering was about me, Jenny, Jenny the fool.

After the Pierces left that night, I asked Heather, "So, did you dye your hair black because of this . . . witch thing?"

At the moment, Heather was retrieving the vodka from the window seat, but as she straightened she snapped, "You were *staring* at it just then, weren't you? My hair?" She pulled a strand in front of her face, gave it a stern, reproving look. "Don't you think I know it's terrible? *Merde!*"

Her chin wobbled. All my life, I've been unable to watch another person cry without beginning to cry myself. Quick, I dropped down on my knees in front of Heather's chair. "Mugs!" I said. "Come on, Mugs, your hair's fine!"

Mugs was what Heather used to call me when she thought I was angry with her. Laughing, and, in a gangland accent, she'd plead, "Mugsie! Don't kill me, Mugs! You know I didn't mean nuttin'!"

"Here, Mugs. Here you go." I picked the candy dish up off the kitchen table and started to pass it back and forth like smelling salts beneath Heather's nose, but she jumped out of her chair, knocking me onto my heels.

"Everybody but you believes I'm a witch, Jenny! Everybody!" She started toward the stairs, then held out a hand to stop me from following. "Just . . . wait here," she said.

In the old days, not wanting to waste a minute of our time together, Heather and I had even accompanied each other on trips to the bathroom. I felt sad, alone in the kitchen, and so I assigned myself a bit of business: found the appropriate bag in the cupboard, refilled the candy dish, though my tongue was already sore from the lemon drops' sugary grit.

"Look." Heather stood in the kitchen doorway. In one hand she held her coat, in the other a naked Ken doll. The doll's legs had been sawed off at the knees, and several nails hammered inexpertly through its bare chest, but I recognized it immediately as one of the dolls that Heather and I had sworn to save for our children—who, we had assumed, would also be best friends.

Heather ran her thumb over the worn flocking on the doll's head.

"The Middlemists helped me make it for Mike Lichtenberg. We'll leave it on his doorstep on our way back."

I knew Heather had been hanging around with the Middlemists, a pair of giggly twins. I was surprised, however, that she knew Mike Lichtenberg well enough to make him a voodoo doll. I had once tried to fall for Mike: tall, handsome, with the sort of black glasses moviemakers always stick on a male face to suggest intelligence. Mike Lichtenberg was not intelligent. Mike was simple as a soft drink ad. No. Simpler. Simple as the soft drink itself. The only time I really cared for him was when he caught me in a lie and repentance added a whiff of complexity to a few of our encounters.

"Why Mike Lichtenberg?" I asked.

With little upward yanks—pop, pop—Heather removed the doll's arms from their sockets. "Why Mr. Spit-in-Your-Mouth-When-He-Kisses-You?" she asked, then tossed what remained of the doll on the table.

I laughed, raised the doll to my eye as if it were a telescope; through its hollow middle, I watched as Heather deposited the arms in the trash basket under the sink, then rummaged through a pile of folded-up grocery sacks, all the while complaining because each sack featured the market's smiling, freckled Jack and Jill, and how could she deliver a voodoo doll in something so absurd?

The truth: the idea of Heather's kissing a boy I had once kissed bothered me. I have to admit that I was distressed by the notion that it might signal her catching up to me in the world of romance. Also: Why hadn't she told me about it? Did she like Mike Lichtenberg? Had she hoped he would call back and he hadn't?

Heather was not saying.

By that point in my life, of course, I understood love could be shameful, force all kinds of words underground. Just a few minutes later, as Heather and I drove across the snowy town—the streets empty, white, quiet as dawn—we passed right by the Lighthouse Motel and I didn't mention to Heather that it had been at the Lighthouse that I'd gotten my heart broken by Andy Rainier.

On and on, that heartbreaker Andy had talked: we couldn't see each other anymore, I was too intense, he didn't even know if he'd come back to the college next quarter. While he talked, I plucked at the meaty edge of the motel's chenille bedspread. I stared at the painting of a canal scene that hung on the motel wall. An earlier guest had enriched the painting with stick figures toting flamethrowers and machine guns. Other stick figures, burning, fell through the Venetian sky. Tiny balloons attached to the figures contained the words "Help, help!" and "I'm on fire!"

Such a pretty boy, with his golden brown hair and cocker spaniel eyes, his laugh that rang out in yelps and groans. A complete stranger, Andy Rainier had walked right up to Heather and me the day we attended his college's little winter festival. He poured a shot of rum into the cup of cocoa in my hand and said to Heather, "I'm in love with your friend, here." He loved me without even knowing me, which, at the time, seemed miraculous; and then, a year later, he knew me and didn't love me, and what could be worse than that?

Heather said, "Stay on Lake Shore Drive, Jen. There'll be a road between the marina and the trailer courts that's supposed to be the fastest way to the spot where the car went off."

I nodded. I tried not to be glum. My mother's Buick felt nice and warm, didn't it? Heather and I were together again. Between us sat an unopened bag of lemon drops and the rest of the bottle of vodka, insurance against the lonely night.

"Listen, Heather," I said, and, then—suddenly shy—invented a little itch on my neck that I paused to scratch. "I wasn't going to tell anybody this, but, you know, because of what you told me . . . well, I guess I have powers, too. I may be a witch, too."

Heather turned to stare at me. "You can't be a witch, too, Jenny." She shook her head, hard. "I bet this has something to do with Andy, doesn't it?"

"No," I said. "He's just . . . the proof, that's all. See, I never *told* anyone, but I've been doing this thing, at night, where I send him, you know—"

I stopped. To my surprise, I was ashamed to say "love" in front of Heather, afraid she'd scoff at the word.

"I send him messages," I said. "Like, I imagine a beam of light carrying a message to him, and when I ran into him at that tire place—I told you? Last week?"

She nodded without looking my way.

"He said he *knew* what I was doing, Heather."

Face covered by a ski mask that had made him appear both preposterous and scary, almost amphibious, the beautiful Andy Rainier had zoomed his motorcycle into the lot of General Tire, right up to the bay where I stood waiting for someone to work on my father's car. I couldn't speak right away. I'd had a queer sensation of invisibility ever since Andy's good-bye, and seeing him again made me feel even stranger, as if I'd resumed some sort of form, but too fast. There he was in that crazy mask—which was just as well since I'd never been able to locate the wellspring of my love for him anywhere more precisely than in his face. Through the orange and black lips of the ski mask he said, "All right, Jenny. I don't know what you're up to, so you tell me. You've been . . . calling to me or something, right? At night? Sending me messages or something?"

From her perch in the passenger's seat, Heather groaned at my account: "Oh, well!" She tucked her legs up beneath her as if she were at home on a couch, then turned to stare out her window.

I felt stung by the dismissal and so didn't tell the rest of my story: How, in that parking lot, I had said, "All it is, is that I love you, Andy," because maybe I had powers, and maybe I didn't, and if they couldn't make him love me, forever and ever, then they weren't worth any more to me than the sparks that flew up when I straightened my covers in the night.

And what did Andy Rainier say to me in closing—this boy with his lovely face covered by terrible red and purple zigzags, orange arrows, the kind of multiple eyes savages have been known to don to keep the devils away? "Knock it off, Jenny. You understand? You got to knock it off, right now."

At the time, it struck me as extraordinary that a young man who could be disappointed that his girlfriend didn't produce noisier orgasms—communicate her relish through back-raking and bites— that this young man could remain unimpressed by the fact that he could hear that same girlfriend's voice over miles and miles of empty space. Now, of course, I understand. We had different wants. Also, maybe my voice in the night was a little scary. I had not, after all, meant for him to hear me calling. I had hoped that he would imagine that he thought of me all on his own.

~

The snow grew deeper as Heather and I drove farther away from town. The banks were higher than I could ever remember having seen them; eight, ten feet in some places, on and on, deep and pure and beautiful as canals cut in white stone. We could have been driving in a riverbed on the face of the moon.

One of several letters I composed in my head as I drove that night, never sent:

> Dear Andrew,
>   Are you happy now? Does your back look like hamburger?

Heather had turned around in her seat again by the time we were halfway to the trailer courts. "Maybe we shouldn't drive out there, after all, Jen. Maybe the roads are just too awful."

I shrugged as if I'd hardly noticed the roads. "Why don't you open those lemon drops?" I said. "Let's have a drink."

Heather tore open the candy bag for me, then leaned it up against the side of my leg. "I don't want anything, though," she said. She closed her eyes and set her chin on the dash, the way a big dog does sometimes—a shepherd, a retriever. "That's the worst part of you and Andy breaking up: no more dope."

"Nice," I said. "Thanks."

She didn't open her eyes when she responded. "Oh, please, Jen. How do you expect me to feel about you guys breaking up? I mean, it's not like you ever even *tried* to call to me, did you? Like you called to him?"

I was startled to a ridiculous degree—you would have thought she'd asked if I'd ever wanted to make love to her—but before I could think of an answer, she said, all in a rush:

"It's too bad you didn't, because if you had—if you'd gotten through, then I'd know whether to believe whether you have powers or not."

Feebly, I offered, "I could try now, if you want."

"God! *No*. Anyway, we've talked about it, it wouldn't count."

I knew I had been a lousy friend. Again and again, I had canceled plans with Heather if Andy Rainier called at the last minute for a movie, a dance, even an ice cream cone. Still, just then I was feeling more anger than remorse. All I really wanted to do was point out that I had better proof of my powers than Heather had of hers; that accidents happened day in, day out—

Instead, I just drove faster, scarcely slowing at all to turn onto the little road carved out between the marina and the trailer court.

Heather yelped—maybe I did too—as the Buick made some dreamy swerve, knocking a load of powder off a bank before I got us straightened out again.

"Jen," Heather gasped, "God, we can't drive up this road!"

I grinned and shoved the bag of candy across the seat. "You should try these. They're the best yet: sweet and sour and salty, too."

"Stop!" Heather's hands gripped the dash so hard she looked as if she might tear it off, throw it at me. "Are you crazy? Turn around."

My stomach fluttered—she was better than I at showing anger outright—but I managed to smile, say, "No place *to* turn around."

The big snowbanks swallowed the trailer court in an instant. We passed a boarded-up hatchery, and then the backside of a series of greenhouses—one of them lit up, revealing a tremendous plant, leaves large as platters pressing against the glass roof. It was the greenhouses that made me realize I had been out that way in the past. During the years before he left for college, my big brother Max had loved to suddenly turn off a main road and drive me down deserted lanes, terrify me with his immediate transformation into a variety of freaks. He did this frequently, but I never seemed to be able to prepare myself for the moment; whenever he started in, it seemed absolutely possible that a person might be your brother one moment and a drooling madman the next.

A terrible, low growling—that was one way Max began. The two of us would be coming home from the skating rink, say, or maybe he'd picked me up at Girl Scouts. I'd hear the growl, or realize that Max now bobbed his head in a frantic, broken-necked sort of way as the car weaved back and forth across the road. "Jenny," Max whispered. "Oh, my god, Jenny! I think . . . I think . . . I think I'm losing my mind!" Something like that. Pretending to be spastic, retarded, possessed. He leered, he rolled his eyes. Ropes of spit hung from his lips. He never stopped until I started to cry.

"Jenny," Heather said, making her voice as flat as possible. "I'm *waiting* for you to turn around."

Wall-eyed, slack-jawed, drooling, I tipped my head toward her shoulder and I mumbled, "Wha? Who you? What you do in my car, li'l girl?"

I was not, however, my brother. I was a drunk girl driving fifty-nine miles an hour on a road no wider than a back alley, a girl who wanted, simultaneously, to win back and punish her friend, and when Heather Pierce looked my way, then lowered her head to her knees and began to shriek in what I immediately recognized as real terror, "Stop! Stop the car!" I did.

That car was big, with plenty of weight; still, it fishtailed, and when it finally came to a stop, it blocked the narrow road, front end touching one snowbank, rear end the other.

Right away, I began to apologize: "I'm sorry, I was just fooling around, come on, Heather," but she was already out the door, taking off at a run.

Few things in my life have frightened me more than the way my face frightened Heather Pierce that night: To be the cause of such terror! Nothing on earth seemed so pressing as to stop Heather's being afraid of me, *now,* so I could stop being afraid of *myself.*

"Please!" I scrambled from the car and shouted to her over the hood, "It's just me! Come back!"

Heather was already a way up the road, but she stopped. She didn't actually look my way, but shouted in a voice both angry and impatient, "I know it's you, dummy! But you're *bleeding!* You're bleeding out of your mouth!"

The words scared me right up to the edge of tears. Blood? Out of my mouth? I hesitated, then swiped my fingers across my chin. They came away wet and dark in the moonlight.

"I *told* you I was a witch!" Heather shouted. "And you didn't believe me, did you?"

Once I understood that she was implying she had cursed me, I stopped being afraid of myself and, out of some dim sense of self-preservation, made myself laugh. What a laugh—big and absolutely phony. Still, the fact that I was able to produce it at all gave me hope and cleared my head.

"Hey." I spit out the lemon drops in my mouth. Roped with blood and saliva, they landed in the snow at my feet. "It's just the *candy.* The candy . . . it's like it sanded my tongue."

Heather didn't come any closer. I shrugged and laughed as if it were all the same to me, the whole matter was just funny. Then I walked over to one of the banks and took a handful of snow into my bloody mouth.

From where I stood, the moonlit fields looked much the way the lake had from Heather's kitchen—the smooth expanse, the margins suggested by trees—but not twenty yards away, the snow had been disturbed. A tangle of lumpy furrows in the snow ran down into the ditch and across a broken section of barbed wire fencing, and I realized that these were the marks left behind by the vehicles that had retrieved Kevin Hammersmith and his car.

Death, I thought, as if I might summon it a little closer, learn a secret or two; but, then, immediately, I felt uneasy and called out, "Here, Heather, I think this is what you wanted to see."

After a moment, I heard the creak of Heather treading on the snow, then the tapping of her shoes on the Buick's bumper as she made her way between the snowdrift and the hood of the car to my side of the road.

I didn't want to look at her any more than she wanted to look at me and, side by side, neither of us talking, we stood staring out at the tracks as if we imagined they might arrange themselves into some pattern, spell out a message we could carry away.

"I should have worn boots," Heather said finally. Very matter-of-fact. Like one of our mothers. "How am I supposed to go out there without boots?"

We both started to shiver; it was not so cold, really, but there seemed no point in staying longer. I opened the door on my side of the car and signaled for her to crawl across the seat.

"One thing," she said, after I'd started the engine, "just because *you* think you're a witch doesn't mean *I'm* not one, too."

I nodded. "I know that. And I'm sorry about scaring you, Heather."

A stupid thing for me to say, I realize now, and no doubt infuriating: my forgetting so fast that what had scared her had been her belief in some curse she had laid on me, and not my pretending to be a lunatic.

"Also," she said, "don't humor me. I know a few things: I know if Andy had called tonight, you wouldn't be with me at all."

I made no more response to this than to release an exasperated breath of air; then I busied myself with the tedious process of straightening out the car, inching it back and forth between the banks. She was right, of course. I had shown her my very own poems. I had sung old Broadway scores with her. I had never felt as easy and happy in the company of anyone as I had with Heather, and—barring my own children—I never have since; yet, I would have abandoned her, again and again, for another night of being reflected in Andy Rainier's eyes.

With almost theatrical caution, I drove us back to Heather's house. We didn't speak of anything, let alone of delivering the voodoo doll to Mike Lichtenberg, and while I was in the Pierces' kitchen, calling home to tell my mother that I wouldn't be staying overnight, after all, I saw Heather stuff the doll into the trash basket beneath the sink.

Not long afterward, Mike Lichtenberg went to Vietnam. He didn't get injured, at least not physically. I saw him at a Christmas party once, a couple of years later, when I was home from college. He insisted on telling a story about how he'd cut off the head of a Vietcong and stuck it on a spike outside his tent as a combination trophy/good luck charm. The crowd at the Christmas party seemed to be about equally divided between those who laughed at the gesture, those who found it appalling, those who thought it made good sense.

Mike Lichtenberg. Andy Rainier. I hardly ever think of the boys I knew back then, but Heather Pierce I think of often. Heather Pierce appears in my dreams with distressing regularity and there she greets me without enthusiasm. She torments me by pretending—in my dreams, I *know* she is pretending—that we never really were such good friends, or if we were, all of that happened far too long ago to really matter to anyone.

A New Life

I T WAS DAVIS who saw the car first. Later, for a little while, I'd say, "I looked down in the ditch and thought I saw something in the snow," which of course gave the impression I was the one, but Davis saw the car first.

If Bailey and I had gone out alone that night, we'd have driven by. I thought about that a lot in the years after, how the littlest thing could make all the difference, turning your head this way instead of that at one moment in your life could decide who you married or whether you lost control on a curve and so on.

That night, we'd been celebrating. Bailey had drawn a low number in the lottery, but just that morning he'd found out his deferment for med school had gone through. None of us was stinking drunk, but we were feeling good, driving back from the city to the little town where our college sat.

In winter, I always counted the last stoplight out of the city as a landmark because, once we got there, I could switch on the heater and we'd finally get warm air. I drove a VW back then. The heater cooked your feet but this was Iowa in January. The windchill could hit fifty below, so we felt grateful for anything.

Just past that stoplight, you came upon some acreages with nice houses, and it was about there that Davis started telling us a story about how his uncle shot a ceramic lawn deer once. He sat forward in the backseat so his chin dug into my shoulder. Davis always had to be doing something like that to me, just to drive me a little crazy.

"The deer shattered, so my uncle knew pretty fast what he'd done. Before he could get away, though, the lady who owned the thing came out, screaming." Davis hooted and kicked at the back of my seat. "All she had on was a bra and panties, man!"

I thought Davis would go on to tell how the lady decided she wasn't mad after all and invited his uncle in to screw. Most of Davis's stories went down that path. Bailey had warned me not to room with him, but, second semester, I was trying to start my life over. I'd been ditched by this girl, and Davis looked like a guy in an underwear ad; he had a big jaw and he stood around a lot with his arms folded so his biceps popped out. I thought, Hey, a good-looking guy like Davis, maybe he'd bring me luck.

Anyway, the story about the lawn deer: it turned out the lady tackled Davis's uncle so hard she rattled his pacemaker. The uncle almost died, she had to call an ambulance, and so on.

Davis told a lot of lies, but I believed that story about his uncle. I remembered it, maybe because of what happened that night, or maybe because—it seems this way to me now—it really did say something about the way people's lives get tangled up with each other.

∽

Outside the city, the road turned curvy and nice. There were lots of trees on the right, up where the houses sat, and snowy fields to the left in long, clean stretches that made me feel whatever had gone wrong in my life could be fixed because life was big and great. I let the car make a little slide, and thought about the girl who'd thrown me over. Elaine Sellen. Black hair. Pale, perfect skin. I was crazy about her. All of first semester, we did everything together: movies and parties and Sunday breakfast at the truck stop after making love most of Saturday night. Sometimes I even let her drag me to hear people read poems or into the city for an opera. Then one night, just before Christmas break, we're sitting in the dining hall, finishing our coffee, and she tells me she's not going to see me anymore. She smiled while she talked. I guessed she didn't want people to know what went on, so I smiled, too. Maybe that was a mistake. I was twenty-one. What did I know? I backed away from the table, mumbled something, "Hey, that's cool, Elaine."

I couldn't remember anything ever hurting me that way—and I felt like a little kid, like when my dad used to beat me up: hurt and afraid, and not just because the beating hurt. Afraid because I wanted to hit back.

That night in January, though, driving along with Bailey and Davis, I started imagining how glad I'd be if Elaine came into the dining hall and sat down with me at breakfast. It'd all been a mistake, she'd say, and we'd spend the whole day making love. She'd have on some opera, and if we got hungry she'd get this box of chocolates from her desk. She was the only girl I ever knew who bought herself boxes of fancy candy. As soon as she finished one, she went out and bought another, like somebody giving herself a gift, you see? She had all kinds of things she did that nobody else at the school did. She took long walks back before that sort of thing caught on. And her room was always freezing because she kept her windows open. She said it was good for us. "Isn't this wonderful?" she'd say. About the cold room, the walks, some lecture we'd been to. "Isn't this wonderful, Todd?"

Anyway, at about that point in Bailey and Davis and my drive, the road curved hard. You had to be careful because the road hugged a bluff—ice built up there, and you could only guess at what lay ahead. If someone came around the bend in your lane, you might end up going off what was a pretty steep bank for that part of the world.

"*Oye,* Todd!" Bailey said, and while I slowed us down, he went into this pretend-Spanish act. Bailey was a great guy. Not bad-looking, but he wore these transparent pink glasses that were really meant for athletics. Bailey thought everybody should wear glasses like that since the plastic was almost unbreakable. This pretend-Spanish thing Bailey did drove Davis wild, mostly because Davis couldn't tell if we knew the language or not. Bailey'd say something like: "Hota con lavaba roota, Todd?" Basically, I'd just work at not laughing.

In the backseat, Davis went on about what fools we were, what jerks, what total nobodies, but then all of a sudden he started in: We had to stop! He'd seen something over the bank!

I slowed down, but not much. Davis loved to tell people—especially girls—stories in which I looked like a fool: Todd walks out of the bathroom attached to the toilet paper roll. Todd screams when a lab rat mysteriously crawls across his mouth at four o'clock in the morning.

"I don't see anything, Davis."

Davis laughed. "What's the matter, Mr. Wonderful? Don't want to get your penny loafers wet?"

He kept it up the whole fifteen miles back to the college. Bailey was quiet. He could be quiet, but his quiet then was a judgment on me, and I was mad enough at both of them that when I brought the car up in front of the student union, I braked so hard, all three of us flew forward a little.

"Jesus, Todd," Bailey said.

I found Davis's face grinning in the rearview mirror. "Will you shut up if I go back?"

He set his chin on my shoulder again. "Scout's honor," he said in what was supposed to sound like some sexy girl's voice.

~

The car was a dark station wagon, rammed into brambles at the base of the ditch.

Davis got out even before I parked, and he went sliding down the bank. "There's a guy in here!" he shouted.

"Look, Todd," Bailey whispered, "even if he's lying, it's good you drove back."

Davis wasn't lying, though. Inside the station wagon, a heavyset man slumped over the wheel.

"What'd I tell you?" Davis danced around in the snow. "Smell the booze!"

I pushed the man down on the seat. His skin was a milky blue, his lips and cheeks cold. I started mouth-to-mouth and, behind me, Davis was going, "I noticed you turned the car around when you parked, Todd. So it'd seem like you stopped the first time, right?"

I didn't know if he was right or wrong. "For Christ sakes, get some help," I said.

I didn't mean both of them, but both of them took off in the VW. I pounded the guy's chest a couple of times. When I did the breathing, my mouth brushed against a little mustache he wore. I'd never done mouth-to-mouth on a person, just a doll. There's some difference, believe me, in a real old guy with big black pores and whiskers and scotch on his breath. Every once in a while, I spooked and reared away from him, afraid if he came around, he'd be a man returned from the dead, more powerful than anything human, burning to eat me alive. Once I heard a car coming, and I scrambled up to the shoulder, trying to get the driver to stop. I suppose I looked like a maniac. The driver almost spun into the ditch, speeding on ice to get away.

Bailey and Davis ended up driving to what turned out to be the house of the guy from the accident. The woman there wouldn't let Davis and Bailey inside, but she said she'd call an ambulance. Then, when they started giving her information about the station wagon, she fainted. She had the door locked, so they couldn't help her *or* use the phone, and finally Davis had to drive to another house to call.

By the time they got back to me, and the ambulance arrived, I was shaking with cold. The police gave me coffee. They didn't say anything about the fact that we'd been drinking. One cop told us he figured the guy—Mr. Bernard—had been in the ditch since before dark, or else he would have turned on his headlights. If he'd had on lights, somebody would have seen the car down there.

"So maybe we drove by him on our way *into* the city?" I asked. The cop nodded, which made me feel a little better. He also said he'd picked up Bernard on that stretch before. He figured this time Bernard had passed out and just driven over the bank. There weren't any signs he'd slid, or tried to stop himself.

~

The next morning, Davis woke me up by rattling the newspaper in my face. I suppose I knew Mr. Bernard wouldn't make it, but, still, it shook me to learn he was dead.

Davis followed me down to the bathroom. Even when I turned the shower on and stepped inside, he stayed, reading me details about the guy. "Served in World War II! Born in England!"

A freshman came in to shave and after showing him the newspaper article and letting him know I'd given Mr. Bernard mouth-to-mouth, Davis brought the guy to my stall and pulled back the curtain: "A man who has tasted death!"

I laughed, then pulled the curtain shut, pumped soap from the dispenser into my washcloth, and scrubbed my mouth.

"So what do you think?" Davis watched me towel off as if I were suddenly a fascinating person. "Was Bernard dead already when you worked on him, Toddy?"

As if I considered him too goofy to deal with, I started down the hall. Bailey stood outside our room, rubbing the bridge of his nose, looking upset.

"That poor lady," he said as he followed us inside. "We ought to go to the funeral, you know?"

Davis smiled at me. "Todd's going to have to think about that," he said; then he started doing sit-ups—always the hard way: upper torso dropped down over the side of the bed.

Bailey was a nicer guy than I was, but at the time I imagined something else, and I said how we'd probably be an unpleasant reminder to the widow, blah, blah, blah, and, in the end, Bailey went to the funeral alone.

~

A few days later, the college newspaper ran a story about the accident. Bailey had given an interview to some girl, and he'd made me out to be a hero. I didn't mind at first—I thought Elaine might hear the news and think well of me—but after a while the attention started to get to me, particularly if Davis were around. One day, this freshman and his girlfriend came up to talk to us at lunch. The girl stared at me like maybe I had chunks of the corpse on my lips, and Davis sat there, giving me these little winks. "Sure, Todd," he said, "tell them what it was like." I was eating a Reuben sandwich, and I said, "It was like this," and I opened up my mouth. Can you believe that? I *opened* my mouth and showed them the chewed-up toast and corned beef and sauerkraut. I was shook, but I acted like it was pure disgust, and I threw down the sandwich and left.

Eventually, of course, I had to go back to the dorm, and there was Davis, sitting at his desk, grinning. "The dead guy's wife called Bailey, Toddy. She invited us for dinner, and he said yes."

~

Bailey assumed he'd remember how to find the house; when we got there, though, it was a different time of day and, on our first try, we ended up at the house where Davis had called for the ambulance. I felt hopeful—maybe we could skip the whole thing—but Bailey got directions and we drove on.

Mrs. Bernard looked like one of those people you used to see advertising tonics for the elderly; not really so old, but wearing wire rims and gray hair and old lady's shoes with fat heels and laces. Weird. Maybe she was younger than Mr. Bernard and she'd tried to look his age. Anyway, our coming to see her made her happy. She acted like a kid giving a tea party, jumping up and down to get things, spilling her water glass. She wanted to know where we all came from and what we studied and so on. It wasn't until we went to the living room that she actually said anything about her husband.

"That's Robert." She pointed to a photograph on the coffee table: a young serviceman who didn't even look like he was related to the old man from the accident—a fact I found pretty depressing in itself.

"And you waited with him, Todd?"

While I nodded, and explained I'd tried to revive him, Davis stood behind Mrs. Bernard's chair, grinning at me like we were in cahoots, and I was getting away with murder.

"See here." Mrs. Bernard got up and took out an atlas so she could show us the spot where Mr. Bernard had been born. "Before I knew Robert," she said, "I always thought people put on British accents to sound high and mighty! Robert wasn't like that at all. I wish you could have known him, boys. A lovely man. He saw a great deal of suffering during the war. Many dear friends died. I think he drank to forget. I tried to help him to stop, of course. I hope . . . maybe there's a lesson for you. About the drinking . . ."

She looked each of us in the eye, as if she wanted to make sure she got a solemn nod out of each of us, and she did. Then she took us on a tour of his homemade lamps: one made of driftwood, another from a jar of marbles, that sort of thing. There was this brass one, too, and she lifted it up so we could see the base was actually a bell.

Bailey asked about it, and she explained the bell had come from the town where Mr. Bernard had grown up. As a small boy, he had heard that very bell sound the warning for air raids during World War I.

Bailey gave me a look like I should say something, too, and so I made some dumb remark, like, well, you'd never know there was a bell there, would you?

That made Davis roll his eyes, but Bailey and Mrs. Bernard nodded and looked as if I'd said just the right thing.

∼

About a week later, Davis and I were in the dining hall, and he caught me looking at Elaine Sellen. I'd never talked to him about Elaine, but he knew I'd dated her, and he said to me, just like I'd asked him to help me scheme something, "I know that Patty she's with. How about if I convince them to play Ping-Pong? Then you show up and make it doubles?"

It surprised me he wanted to help me out, but I didn't object. From where I sat the conversation looked promising. Elaine even glanced my way a couple of times. But when Davis came back, he shook his head: "She's got other plans, Todd."

He watched my face so hard I wondered if he'd done the whole thing just for my reaction. I shrugged as if I hadn't expected anything, but I'd gotten my hopes up, and it was hard to go back to where I'd been.

The next day, after class—just to get away from Davis and the school—I decided to go over to the car wash and clean off the salt I'd picked up over the winter. It was really warm out, the campus all sloppy with melting snow, and, first, I stopped by the dorm to change into my old shoes. The message bolt was down in the room so I checked Davis and my box.

Todd—
Call Elaine 695-3981.

I was so happy, I wanted to let out a big whoop and run right over to her dorm. I didn't do it, of course, but I did go straight down the hall to the phone.

An older woman answered. The house mother, I thought. I said who was calling, then asked for Elaine.

"You mean *Ellen!*" The woman laughed. "This is Ellen *Bernard*, Todd. Someone must have taken the message wrong!"

To make a long story short, Mrs. Bernard wanted us to come for dinner again. I was so screwed up about the mistake with the message, I hardly knew what I was saying for an excuse, some sort of TV version of campus complications: big test, blah, blah, dorm meeting, blah, blah, blah.

"Yes, well, I understand, dear," she said.

I forgot about washing off the car after that. I just drove to the Jack and Jill and got myself a case of beer, took it with me out to the palisades, drank through dinner.

When I got back to the room, Davis and some freshman were on my bed. That was another thing about him: he liked to make out with girls on *my* bed. Her shirt was unbuttoned, and I started backing out the door, but he goes, no, no, and tells the girl to leave, the two of us have to get down to studying.

Davis didn't ever drink much. "I prefer watching the rest of you fall on your faces," he always said. That's what he did that night. At first, I just drank and he talked. Mrs. Bernard had called him, too. He said something crude about the call, like she probably wanted us to come jump her bones, did I think maybe that's what Bailey was doing, jumping her bones? Then he talked about the freshman and some other girls he'd had sex with from the college.

I was pretty smashed and for some insane reason I started talking about Elaine. I didn't say she was the only girl I'd ever had sex with, which was the truth. I just said how great she was in bed, that sort of thing. I wasn't real specific, or anything, but when I saw Bailey standing in our doorway, I guess I flinched.

"Todd." Bailey came right in and pulled me to my feet, kind of giving me a shake in the process. "Let's go to the Rat, and get you something to eat."

The Rat. That's what they called the snack bar at the union.

A lot of snow and ice had melted that day, but things cooled off at dark and it felt good to get inside after crossing campus. The Rat had a seating pit around a fireplace—the sort of thing people thought was cool when they toured a campus—and the three of us sat down there. Davis and Bailey talked about guitar players. I was too wrecked to join in. I just laughed. As if it made some difference who we liked best. Up at the jukebox, two girls kept putting on songs, sad ones that made my drunkard's heart swell. I had a nutty idea in those days that if I just *felt* bad enough, Elaine and I would somehow start all over again, and so I hunkered down in my parka and worked on my sadness, all the while getting dreamier, dopier. I'd almost gone under completely when I felt something in the air, almost like a slap, and I opened my eyes.

There she stood. She had on a red ski jacket and a matching set of blue fur earmuffs and mittens that would have looked silly on anybody, but made her look like something out of a fairy tale.

She was talking to Bailey. "Ron told me about you guys finding that person," she said. Ron was Davis's first name. It gave me the creeps to hear his name in her mouth.

Bailey said some stuff back: how he felt sorry for Mrs. Bernard, and how Mr. Bernard probably would have lived if he hadn't been drinking when he went in the ditch. Then he jerked his head in my direction, signaling I should slide down the seating pit, get closer to the conversation.

Elaine glanced over at me, then looked back at Bailey as if I were some stranger. I stayed put. "He probably wouldn't have *gone* in the ditch if he hadn't been drinking," she said.

Then Bailey told her how I'd tried to revive Mr. Bernard, and so on. I waited for Davis to make a few wisecracks about that, but Davis just sat with the back of his head pressed against the wall of the pit: he looked like a movie star playing a political prisoner or a philosopher.

Every now and then, while Bailey talked, Elaine looked my way. He was still saying something to her when she walked over to me and sat down. Her face was pink, she looked almost as if she might cry. "I just want to tell you," she murmured, "Ron told me the real story, and I think what you did that night—driving by that car—I think it stinks."

Bailey didn't know what went on between us. He looked up from his bag of barbecued potato chips and smiled at Elaine and me like we were a pair of lovebirds.

My brain was straw, I was like the Scarecrow in *The Wizard of Oz.* "I thought Davis was *lying* about there being a car," I said.

She shook her head. "Look at you!" She'd raised her voice loud enough that people turned, and I did what plenty of people do when they feel awkward. I grinned.

I'd never seen her mad. We hadn't fought when we were together, but just then the tip of her nose was pure white. She brought her face so close that I could feel her breath when she whispered, "You aren't a serious person, Todd."

It wasn't as if she meant I was goofy; it was more like she meant I wasn't quite *real*, and I hated her for that. I wanted to hit her, or hold her head under water, the same way I'd wanted to back in December, and, quick, to get hold of myself, I grabbed a log and threw it on the fire.

What'd I know about fires? I was drunk and crazy. My log crashed into a log that already burned. A few good-size embers flew right onto the pit's carpet. Across the way, a bunch of people jumped up, and a couple guys shouted at me: "Jesus!" "Be cool, man!"

Be cool. I stomped out the sparks. I sat down again. Elaine was gone, and I didn't so much as look around the room to see where she'd gone. Just sat and watched the fire, and the next thing I knew, someone was tapping me on the shoulder.

"You all right, dear?" A chubby-cheeked lady in a matted overcoat, fake corsage on the lapel, leaned over me. One of the snack bar ladies, framed by the gray morning light coming in the window.

My heart pounded: something about being left alone in that place all night, locked in at closing, no one—not even me—realizing I was there.

The snack bar lady brought me a carton of orange juice and—grateful to the point of tears, my head aching with beer—I drank it down while she watched.

Overnight, the snow and ice that had melted the day before had refrozen and walking to Bailey's dorm was like crossing a field of doorknobs. Still, you could tell the day would warm by noon. Everything felt damp, and a mist hung around the evergreens and the campus grounds, which dipped here and there, the way college grounds were supposed to.

Bailey didn't say a word about leaving me at the Rat. He played me flute music recorded in the Taj Mahal and, without my even asking, poured three aspirin into my palm.

"Anything transpire with Elaine?"

"Elaine thinks I'm scum. Davis told her how I drove by Mr. Bernard the first time."

"Oh, well. You had your reasons."

"Yeah. I didn't want to look like a jerk."

While Bailey shaved, I stood by a window and listened to the flute thing, and then some old Wes Montgomery. People started straggling out of the union from breakfast, then a lot of them left in a rush, and the sun came out. Finally, I took a big breath, and asked, "So, what's with you guys leaving me at the Rat all night?"

Bailey couldn't have faked the surprise on his face. "I left while you were still talking to Elaine, man. Davis didn't help you get back?"

To show there were no hard feelings, I grinned while I shook my head, then I headed straight out the door for Davis and my dorm. It seemed like the most important thing in the world to me that I immediately convince Davis I hadn't been bothered by his leaving me at the Rat. I didn't want him walking around thinking otherwise for one more *minute* than was necessary, and it made me crazy that he might have already been awake for an hour or two, eaten breakfast with the idea that he'd had some effect on me.

I started walking faster than usual so I could finish with Davis quick, but I felt the way you do in a dream where you're not getting anywhere. The sun was out again, and the melt ran from beneath the sheets of ice that had built up over the winter. There was water crossing the sidewalks in skeins that left me dizzy, and everything was noisy—tires on the wet drives and down in the streets of town, and melt dripping over the tops of the dorm gutters.

I looked ahead to Davis and my dorm, trying to pick out our window, as if I could start avenging myself on Davis before I even arrived. Like I said, I didn't feel I was making much progress, but the window stopped me dead in my tracks.

Over Christmas, my mother had made me some curtains with green and blue stripes, and, that morning, the ends of those curtains were flapping out the window. I noticed because I'd never seen the curtains like that before. Davis and I never slept with our window open. And there was something else. It took me a moment to register the music coming out the window because it wasn't all that loud. *Pagliacci.*

I was standing there in the parking lot, watching the curtains, no idea of what to do next, when Mrs. Bernard called to me.

Actually, I didn't recognize her at first; I was too nuts, I suppose, and she looked older than I remembered, as if her husband's death had settled in. She was smiling, though, picking her way across the parking lot, a big box in her arms. She set the box down on the ground when she reached me. It held three of the homemade lamps she'd shown us the night we'd gone to her house for dinner.

"Now don't think I'm a pest," she said, "but I want to give each of you boys something to remember Robert by." She handed me the bell lamp. "Because you admired it, Todd, and because of your efforts to help."

I kept my eyes on the curtains while she talked about the bell, how I should remember its history, and all.

"I don't know if you can imagine, Todd," she said finally. "I feel not quite right in the head when I think Robert's gone. How could he be dead, and I'll never see him again?"

I understood she was in pain, but I couldn't help myself. I stood up on my toes, dreaming somehow I'd see into that second story without going up the stairs.

"You're heading somewhere," Mrs. Bernard said. "I just wanted to let you know—it was pleasant, having you boys in."

I nodded. Somebody closed the window, gradually pulling the curtains in. For a moment, I felt as if I might black out, but there I stood, and there stood Mrs. Bernard, waiting, and so I went on about some jazz, how time would heal her wounds, and so on.

While I talked, Mrs. Bernard looked off in the direction of the president's house. Like I said, everything was dripping. A lot of birds flapped from the trees over to the power lines strung from the dorm, and back again. I felt as if I had to raise my voice to be heard, and when I finished, Mrs. Bernard just looked tired. She asked if I'd mind taking Davis's lamp up to him myself.

I don't know. At that moment, it seemed to me Davis had *planned* for me to find him with Elaine—arranged things for my personal humiliation—and that Mrs. Bernard and her lamps had come just in time to reflect the garbage back onto Davis and Elaine, make me just a bystander. Which was what I thought I wanted.

"Listen, Mrs. Bernard," I said, "I'm sure Ron would feel bad if he didn't get to thank you for the lamp in person."

~

Afterward, on the way back to the parking lot, Mrs. Bernard walked fast, like she wanted to get away from me, but when we got to her car, she said, "I guess you knew they were there like that, didn't you, Todd?" She sounded mad, but she kept her voice low and people walked past without looking our way.

"That girl . . . you loved her once?"

I shrugged. We both stood there for a moment, not talking, then I gave her directions to Bailey's dorm.

That morning, when she drove past me, Mrs. Bernard lifted one hand in a salute, but she kept her eyes on the driveway. The front end and then the rear of her car dipped as she went over the speed bump. I was surprised that she drove the same car in which Mr. Bernard had died. For a moment, I disapproved of her for driving that car. Actually *disapproved* of her. But you can see how it was for me in those days: I was only just beginning to understand that a person couldn't go out and get a whole new life every time something bad happened to the old one, that the old life and the new life were one and the same.

Suicide's Girlfriend

I

THERE HAD BEEN a suicide. This was in Tucson, Arizona. Early May. As if they knew that drama was in order, the city's ring of mountains brought on a series of outrageous, gut-bright sunsets for those people—not all of them friends of the dead man—who tramped out into the desert or sat on the traffic-blasted patios of that overgrown town's coffeehouses and bars to discuss the matter of his death.

"Wake up, I have something to show you."

The suicide's last words. Spoken to the young woman with whom he lived. He had been young himself. Twenty-seven. A promising future ahead of him.

Everyone knew of adobe bungalows like the one rented by the pair. Built in the thirties. Enough charm that the tenants—many of them students at the university—forgave, or even took pride in, say, a kitchen wall with a crack so wide it allowed in a jagged glimpse of desert sky. Wood floors worn to something like suede. Beehive fireplace. The evaporative cooler that forever dripped over the lip of the roof.

Which made it hard for people *not* to picture the drama, the distraught girlfriend, the mess. Of course, it was shameful to think that way—of gouts of blood, shattered bits of skull, flap of skin, brains.

No letter? No letter.

Someone suggested that the suicide's method might have been inspired by an article that had run in the local paper only days before the death: a human interest piece on a California woman who ran a cleaning service that took jobs no one else would handle. "The worst are shotgun suicides," the cleaning service woman had said. In the accompanying photograph, she wore a white jumpsuit with a red heart stitched on its breast pocket. "We do our best to give the family back their home. It takes me and four trained staff six hours to do a room, and lots of times there's still things—books and special things—that just can't be saved."

II

A large man in a midsize car. A young woman beneath a carport covered in cat's-claw vine. Post–World War II ranch-style house. Modest. Brick. From inside the house, a bird screeched out into the cracked heat of the desert morning. A cockatiel—small, white hybrid with clownish patches of orange on its cheeks. Angry? Heartbroken? Minute talons allowed the cockatiel to cling to the home's screen door while it cried for the young woman in the carport: Candace Cleeve, just then watching Professor Carson O'Connor back his car out the gravel drive.

"One minute, sweetie," Candace Cleeve called to the bird. Impossible to tell that Candace felt ill, but Candace—had Candace been a cockatiel, she, too, would have screeched in despair. The day before, Candace and Carson had fought, and though they had made up, this morning Carson was off on a three-week car trip to the Midwest. In addition to meeting with fellow geologists, he would visit his college-age children, offspring of the marriage he had abandoned in favor of Candace. He would undoubtedly see the children's mother, and the big frame house they had shared on a shady Iowa street. He would, perhaps, feel some regret.

"Self-indulgent?" Carson had roared during yesterday's argument—an ugly thing concerning last week's suicide of one of his graduate students, and Candace's pain at the fact that Carson had spent the entire six days before his trip consoling grieving students over the telephone, meeting with groups of them at "mourning sessions," helping them to set up a memorial picnic, and, finally, attending that picnic for the whole of yesterday afternoon.

"A memorial picnic for a guy who wakes up his girlfriend so she has to see him blow out his brains!" Candace protested during last night's argument. "That makes a hell of a lot of sense!"

Still, Carson was six foot seven inches tall, and every other part of him was equally large—lips, tongue, teeth. Like a tank when it noses over a rim, then begins its grinding descent, Carson suggested the possession of plenty of spooky power; and Candace—who had passed a fair share of her childhood being knocked around by a bored father, had just barely managed to maintain something like a sneer when Carson roared, "*You* are the one who's self-indulgent, Candy!"

Now, however, it was morning and, from behind the wheel of his beige Toyota, Carson smiled benignly at Candace. Candace smiled back, but when Carson and car briefly disappeared behind a hedge of tall and ill-kempt oleander, she gave the nod to those fraternal twins of emotion: fear and relief.

"For you guys to treat this . . . asshole like a hero! It's so self-indulgent!" More of Candace's words from the quarrel. Had it been the first or the second exclamation that triggered Carson's fury? Hard to know where anger began. Perhaps it had sprung up most fiercely when Candace included Carson among the "self-indulgent." Candace knew that Carson was a good man. Candace believed that she herself was the worst thing Carson had ever done. *St. Carson,* Candace sometimes called him, but only in her head, preferring not to provide him additional advantage.

But perhaps she had made Carson most furious when she referred to the student-suicide as an "asshole"? There was no denying that Candace felt a twinge of power and aversion—something physical, almost reflexive—when she pronounced the word. She knew that "asshole" drew a picture—mauve flesh, bitter pucker, central seed of shit and darkness—and that though Carson considered himself a liberal, a "former hippie, for god's sake," he did not like vulgarity. Still, "asshole" was an uncalculated risk on the part of Candace, who tended to be frantic in argument with Carson. Candace, after all, had been born two years *after* Carson graduated from high school. Candace had grown up on what may have been the most wretched of all the wretched little hog farms in all of Iowa, while Carson had his lawyer dad and bridge-club mother and sailboat summers. With "asshole," frantic Candace had pitched a rusty manure fork at Carson and hoped . . . What all did she hope to do with that nasty implement? Well, she was ambitious. She meant to do damage and to enlighten and to pull Carson near.

And apparently she succeeded, something had worked, for now, at the end of the drive, ready to depart for places north and east, Carson called from his rolled-down window, "Hey, Candy! Security, Candy! And don't read the newspaper!" He laughed, then waved his slab of a hand—king-size? colossal?—and drove off down the street.

The first thing that Candace had noticed about Carson O'Connor when he and wife and son appeared beyond the muzzy glass porch that she used as her studio in those days—that is, the first thing she noticed after Carson's spooky height and breadth of bone—was his hair, stiff streaks of both pure black and pure white that stood up like the bristles of a much used housepaint brush. In a man, a bit of the monster could draw a woman on, convince her she was something of a connoisseur. Of course, it was no news that rarely did the converse occur. Candace understood that she had caught Carson's heart with her kiddy-bones, her small cat's face framed by a vaguely Parisian fringe of dark hair—which did not change the fact that she generally saw herself as Poor Iowa Farm Girl, and only occasionally caught a glimpse (as it were, through a crack in the hog-shed walls) of whatever Carson considered her charms.

"Keep the shades drawn." "Don't walk around in your underwear."

"Remember to eat." "Don't tell people you're alone." Things Carson had said while Candace helped him load the car. Candace took such warnings as proof that Carson both cared for her/didn't quite trust her; that he took what he saw as her lack of vigilance for something akin to promiscuity. And so, though she missed Carson already, Candace was also glad to see his big shadow recede from her patch of earth for a while. Gone, Carson could not show up in her studio to take away her paintbrush, remove her clothing; could not offer advice on how to deal with her gallery, or titles for her paintings, and even subjects for future work. Sometimes, the sheer effort of resisting Carson left Candace feeling dull, dull, dull, as if her brain had grown a crisp layer of chitin, some self-defeating means of self-defense.

Still, as she watched the beige Toyota—now waiting at the stop that led to the busy boulevard beyond—her eyes filled with tears, because, after all, she *was* self-indulgent, selfish, awful. Though she had not known the student-suicide, in the first days, she had wanted to talk endlessly about his death, hadn't she? In her sorrow for the girlfriend, Candace had *cried* into the telephone while sharing the story with Joe Raven, her gallery rep in New York, and Candace had met Joe Raven exactly once. Really, until she grew jealous of Carson's involvement in the suicide's aftermath, Candace had even considered telephoning the girlfriend to express sympathy! Snort, snort, snuffle, snuffle. A repellent scene that would have been, Candace felt sure, like something featuring her father, morose on Old Milwaukee.

And didn't she sound revoltingly like her father, now, as she called to the crying cockatiel, "Keep your shirt on"?

"Don't get your ass bent out of shape." "Clean the shit out of your ears."

Really, Candace had never meant to fall in love with a bird any more than she had meant to live in a house with a swimming pool or to ruin someone's marriage, but suppose a certain monumental man announced that he had left his wife for you, and then that man carried you off to Arizona, where every house that the realtor showed you had a swimming pool, and, then, later, while you were out skimming leaves from what had become your very own body of water, a lovely white bird flew down and landed on your head, and that bird needed you? She nuzzled under your chin and cried for you when you went away and no one ever reported her lost in the newspaper: What could you do?

Disturbing, the way that—at the very moment that Carson turned onto the boulevard—his tan car became indistinguishable from all the other light-colored cars on the road.

In the desert, a light-colored car does not show the desert's constant dust so easily as a dark car. A light-colored car reflects heat and can be as much as twenty degrees cooler than one of a dark color.

Candace recited the above to herself as she headed toward the house, the bird. Like so many who make a vocation of seeking the ineffable, Candace had a crush on facts, saw them as surrounded by coronas of suggestion. "Charming!" Carson cried when he had recognized this quality of his love's mind. Carson, however, was a geologist. Carson believed that the real beauty in a thing resided precisely where all speculation regarding its nature could be contained.

"Okay, sweetie, I'm here," Candace murmured to the bird, then paused inside the door in order that her eyes might adjust to the plunge from desert glare to brothy interior. Rose, turquoise: so her temporarily befuddled vision powdered the white feathers of the little cockatiel as it flew with a sweet flutter to her shoulder.

"Want to go paint?" With one hand, Candace smoothed the bird's feathers; with the other, as she passed Carson's desk, she took up the section of newspaper that Carson had snatched away from her that morning.

What had Carson not wanted her to see? While her eyes adjusted to the dim light, she told herself: *Complete dark adaptation—the rods taking over for the cones—requires approximately twenty minutes.* Or was it the other way around? Cones for rods? She could not make sense of the photo that dominated the front page. Gulf War vet addresses students, read the caption, and, yes, there was a figure in dress uniform, but the face was a strange darkness, a whirlwind, a paper wasp's nest. The article explained: The pictured soldier had been trapped in a fire inside his tank. Seventy-five percent of his body had received third-degree burns. He lost his eyelids, his nose, his toes and fingers. Though blind, he now traveled the country, trying to carry a message of inspiration. He was proud he had served, the soldier said, though he did not deny his lot was hard. The last two sentences of the article read, "I'd give up my legs or arms—both—to have back my face. Without my face, it's hard to feel like myself."

Candace clutched the newspaper against her chest. "Jesus. God help you, dear man," she whispered, for though she was not at all sure about God, she supposed the soldier might be, and that she ought to speak on behalf of any possible belief he might possess.

Really, the photo left her feeling so dizzy that out of its ashes rose a happy thought: Maybe I feel this way because I'm pregnant? Carson had had a vasectomy prior to his meeting Candace some three years before, but Candace secretly held out for the possibility of a surgical failure. So perhaps she exaggerated her dizziness and the need to steady herself? To take a seat at Carson's desk?

With woozy care, she set the newspaper next to a sheaf of stapled papers, the top page of which bore a Xeroxed photo of a grinning young man. *Rick Haynes, 1969–1997.* Beneath the photo was information regarding the time and place of the picnic/softball game in Rick Haynes's memory.

A few of the ways that, in her time, Candace had considered killing herself: car crash into telephone poles and/or other inanimate objects; drowning; pills; leaps off surefire bridges or mountainsides. Never, however, had she dreamed of inflicting her suicide upon an audience or using a method whereby she would leave a terrible mess in somebody's home. Never.

"Bastard," Candace murmured to the Rick Haynes photo.

Though she had heard Carson and his colleagues discuss Rick Haynes on several occasions—he came from a wealthy family; he was a mountain climber, brilliant, a drunk, often suicidal—Candace had met Haynes only once. Back in the autumn, very late at night, she had gone to answer the front door and, opening it, found a drunken, bare-chested male ringing the bell and running the garden hose, full tilt, over his head of curly red hair.

"You're Candy?" the young man asked with a laugh. It was not unusual for Candace to feel self-conscious in front of people from Carson's department, all of whom seemed surprised to find that she was Carson's wife. This being the case, when Carson appeared behind her in the hall and led the dripping Haynes out through the living room's sliding doors to the back patio, Candace did not join the pair, but returned to her studio. There, too, sliding doors opened onto the patio and she could overhear the men as she painted.

From their conversation, Candace had gathered that Haynes had just learned that someone had written him a less than glowing grant recommendation. In view of this, Haynes declared he wanted to kill himself. "I'm a piece of shit, Carson! Pure, unadulterated shit!" Not long after this, however, Candace heard Haynes express a desire to go mountain climbing. "Come on, Carson! Or else watch reruns of *Harry O! Harry O*'s great! Or go to Frank's for sausage gravy and biscuits! D'you think Frank's would be open yet? No, Jesus, what am I talking about? I want to fucking kill myself!"

While Haynes had paced the brick patio or rattled around in one of the moldering director's chairs left behind by the home's last own-ers, Carson stretched himself out on the bricks, hands folded behind his head. Candace could not make out much of what Carson said, but now and then she did hear him laugh. Did she make Carson laugh, Candace wondered. She was slightly relieved, a short while later, when Carson brought Haynes to the door of the studio and, grinning, asked if Candace would *please, please recalibrate Rick by singing "I'm a Villain."* "I'm a Villain" was a cheerfully perverse little tune that Candace had learned from a cousin some twenty years before and, paintbrush in hand—eyes fixed upon the studio's pressed-board ceil-ing with its pockmarks from the past owner's games of darts—Candace sang a hurried:

Oh, I'm a villain, a dirty rotten villain,
Stabbing is my favorite form of crime!
My favorite joke is watching people choke,
Stabbing crippled newsboys in the slime!
I'm rough! I'm tough!
I eat meat! Snort! Snort! Raw meat! Beware!

When she finished, she looked out the door and said, "I think there's more, but that's all I know." Rick Haynes laughed and clapped and Carson said, "Thanks, Candy. I think that'll help Rick regain a sense of proportion." Then Carson put his arm over Rick Haynes's shoulder and began to walk him back across the patio, saying as they went, "I've seen you with your students, Rick. You know how to teach, and that's rare!" He went on, then—using words that felt uncomfortably familiar to Candace—to tell Haynes that Haynes had everything to live for. Hadn't Candace received similar words of encouragement from Carson, once upon a time? Hadn't she felt her agreeing to everything he said was a condition she must satisfy before he felt it was safe to love her?

When Haynes finally left the house that morning, it was four o'clock or later. Carson came into the studio. "An interesting guy," Carson said. He pulled up his shirt and began to rub his broad stomach. An assertive, self-pleased gesture. On some occasions, it would have filled Candace with desire. Just then, however, while Candace went through the motions of scraping the table on which she had laid out her paints, her brain erected a swath of distant landscape, a thicket of trees that crinkled, and slumped, and folded in upon itself like a cellophane construction brought too close to flame. She turned from her work and asked—the words tiny things, insect wings, desiccated with her sense of how she disgraced herself—"So, would you think I was more interesting if I were still, you know, suicidal?"

For a time, Carson continued to rub his stomach. Perhaps he had not heard? No. He had heard, and he said, finally, in a voice full of chill disgust, "If being suicidal is just something you can choose to be, then you're not really suicidal, are you, Candy?" He paused. "But if our being married hasn't stopped you from thinking about suicide, maybe we should get divorced."

Robbed. That was how Candace had felt in the dawn of that autumn morning. The possibility of suicide had been the lens through which she saw that her life was all her fortune. If Carson took away the possibility of her even *thinking* about the act . . . why, then, there was no way to see that fortune without losing Carson in the process.

~

Perhaps the cockatiel was distressed by the flapping of the hall window shade that Candace let fly—or perhaps it was the ringing of the telephone—at any rate, the bird sunk her fine nails into the flesh of Candace's shoulder and kept them there while Candace hurried back to the telephone on Carson's desk.

The caller identified herself as one of Carson's students. Had she provided her name, Joyce Burton, Candace almost certainly would have recognized it and realized that the caller was the suicide's girlfriend. In that case, Candace would have had to employ one of her tricks—bite a finger, hard; twist a pinch of skin between her fingernails—in order not to cry, *Oh, I'm so sorry about your loss!* But the caller did not identify herself, and Candace felt merely annoyed at the way that the woman persisted in referring to Carson as "Carson," especially after Candace referred to him as "Dr. O'Connor."

"I wondered if anybody'd be around if I dropped off some books of his."

The caller's voice—that stylized, throaty business favored by certain female disc jockeys—it put Candace off; still, while the woman continued, *Oh, yes, she knew that Carson was off to Iowa,* Candace tried to reason with herself: maybe it was better to have a perfectly fatuous voice as opposed to some dull thing you kept from fear of sounding counterfeit.

"But I may . . . be out this afternoon."

"Would you be back by five, though?"

Squawk, went the cockatiel, as if voicing Candace's reluctance to see the caller. In appreciation, Candace drew a finger down the bird's back; a wonderful thing how, there, the feathers always felt simultaneously warm, cool.

"Was that your bird?" the caller asked. "Yesterday—at the picnic?—Carson told us all about you and your bird."

"Excuse me a moment." Candace placed the receiver on Carson's desk.

A cockatiel is a branch climber. A tame cockatiel will automatically step onto a human finger if that finger is set close to the bird's breast.

In the hall leading from Carson's study to the kitchen stood a little gateleg table and Candace set the bird there, where, for a while at least, the creature would keep company with her bright reflection in the hall mirror. Carson always said that the bird liked mirrors because it was in love with itself, an assertion that caused a cloudy burning in Candace's gut. Candace knew the bird to be finer than that: Candace's bird believed another bird existed in the mirror. It was that other bird that Candace's bird loved.

"Sorry," Candace said to the caller as she took up the receiver again.

"So, does the bird have a name?"

"Oh"—Candace squeezed her eyes shut at the pretension of her own and Carson's choice—"Phoulish Phlame, spelled with Ph's instead of F's. Carson wanted to call her Fool with an F, but I didn't think that was nice, so we came up with this other thing. Actually, Carson says *she's* a *he,* but I heard it hurts to have them sexed, so we just . . . agree to disagree." She took a breath, aware that she rambled: her attempt to prove to the student that she, Carson's wife, did, indeed, exist. "Anyway, she's got a little yellow cockade, like a flame, and I thought Phoulish Phlame sounded like an old love song. Did you ever hear the Ink Spots? One of my professors used to play these old Ink Spot records during studio. 'My Echo, My Shadow and Me.' 'Whispering Grass, Don't Tell the Trees for the Trees Don't Need to Know.'"

The caller gave a little laugh. Did she find Candace entertaining?

Nuts? Candace felt exhausted by the time that she got off the telephone. She laid her cheek on Carson's desk blotter. Indulged in a credible imitation of the caller's throaty voice—"Of course, I know Carson's in Iowa"—before reminding herself that being bitter and envious was surely no better than being aggressive and attention-seeking.

So maybe there was no way to be, at all?

Cheek on the blotter, she lifted the sheet of paper that held the photo of curly-haired Rick Haynes. Maybe he had asked himself the same question.

She sighed, and closed her eyes, then felt a stab of guilt and snapped them open. Because she had not accompanied Carson on his trip, she knew Carson expected her to spend every minute they were apart working on her July show. That very morning, hadn't he plunged his big head into her studio in order to say—very lively— "Hey, Candy, looks like you've got enough food in the cupboards, you won't even have to leave the house while I'm gone"?

Scary but necessary to ask, "Are you trying to tell me I shouldn't go anywhere, Carson?" To which question the big, homely-handsome face expressed grave disappointment. Also, Candace had spied the tanned, leonine face of Carson's ex-wife looking out from Carson's face; the ex would never have accused Carson of scheming. Of course, Candace understood that face was not really the face of Dana O'Connor; maybe not even something rigged up by Carson. Perhaps rigged up by Candace herself? Who knew? Who knew? The notion that you alone invented each of your thoughts and feelings was hot property these days: *What's that you say? I hurt you? No, no, my friend, you hurt yourself!* Without lifting her head, Candace eyed the little digital clock on Carson's desk. 10:47. Had she agreed to the student's coming at five? Six? And should Candace call her parents to tell them that, during his trip, Carson meant to drive his son and daughter over to visit the farm? "Oh, yes," Carson had stoutly declared, "every Iowan ought to know what a genuine pig farm looked like." Candace, however, suspected that Carson actually hoped a tour of the Cleeve farm—all mud and stink and splintered outbuildings—would implant the idea in his children's heads that poor Candace needed their dad far more than their tall, tennis-playing mom ever did. A chancy business, Candace thought. The children, after all, were almost adults and had no particular reason to *need* to like Candace. Suppose the only effect of their visit was to mingle their idea of Candace with a memory of pig shit and stupidity. After all, Carson had been in *love* with Candace on his own first visit to the pig farm. He had been all set to beat up Morley Cleeve for ancient history. Yet Carson came away from his tour as round-eyed as the only kid that Candace had ever dared bring home after school, and, these days, there was even a flush toilet.

"What if that teacher hadn't helped you get a scholarship?" Carson had cried. "My god!" His astonishment both pleased and irritated Candace. She had liked the idea that Carson could not fathom Morley and Georgine as her parents, but also recognized that Carson's failure of imagination was not entirely flattering; fluke, she might be, but Georgine and Morley were her parents, flesh of her flesh. Her whole, half of each.

> *Dear Folks in Earth Science, fellow grad students, faculty, everybody—*
>
> *The week since Rick's suicide has been a time of grief and sharing for all of us. There's been a lot of tears and love around this place. All of you have been great. Special thanks are due to Carson O'Connor for setting up meetings with the grief counselors and getting the department to help with the cost of the picnic. Rick's folks and I are tremendously appreciative to you all, and look forward to the picnic/ball game and the chance to share in remembering what a terrific person Rick really was.*
>
> *Love,*
>
> *Joyce*

This was the second of the stapled Xeroxed pages concerning Rick Haynes. Candace read it without lifting her cheek from Carson's blotter, which had the pleasant effect of making the white spaces between the lines of type into stripes.

Just after the suicide, Carson had reminded Candace—unnecessarily—that she had once met Joyce Burton at an Earth Science party. Candace remembered Joyce Burton quite well. Big. Lumpish. Wearing a collection of rings that looked like pipe fittings, and an outlandishly tight and plunging pink knit that indicated either enormous self-confidence in her appearance or a complete disregard of it. Joyce Burton had sat upon the department chair's kitchen counter and chortled at her own bawdy tale of an encounter with a Nogales street vendor. Standing by herself, pretending interest in the spectacular city views available from the department chair's kitchen windows, Candace had watched Joyce Burton's reflection, and wondered: Did Joyce Burton's confidence come from her hair—which was a truly lovely sheet of icy blonde— or from a sense of being smart or loved, or from money, or what? The showy way in which Joyce Burton seized fellow students and faculty in greeting struck Candace as intriguing, paradoxical: Joyce Burton might have been hoisting onto a cart the great bags of a grain that she required to keep up the strength to hoist great bags of grain onto a cart.

Well, Candace had not gotten off the farm by being stupid. She understood that she envied Joyce Burton. Indeed, because sometimes Candace could not help wanting to be absolutely everyone, in the course of the days since the Rick Haynes suicide, Candace had occasionally—albeit guiltily—caught herself envying Joyce Burton's grief, her starring role as victim/lover/bereaved. Appalling, yes, though not quite so mean when squarely faced. What would have helped, if Carson had been home . . . it would have helped Candace a lot to bring such envy into the light and make it a joke upon herself, like the time that Carson turned up the Toyota's radio to hear a song he had liked as a boy, and Candace was able to poke him and say, "Oh, no, now I have to be jealous of this Girl from Ipanema, too!"

∼

There had been some overlap in the times when both Carson and Candace were at the University of Iowa—she as a student, he as a professor—but the two never met there, and Carson had blushed when, unpacking from their move to Arizona, Candace came upon a packet of photos of Carson as a young professor (the flannel shirt, the woodsman's beard covering face and neck). "My redundant phase," Carson said, "you wouldn't have liked me." Dated 1978, that photo had been a scary reminder to Candace that Carson might well die long before she did; and her voice was clotted when she replied, "I could never *not* have liked you, Carson."

From her own days at the university, Candace owned only one photo: a black and white that the *Des Moines Register* had run with an article on the state's promising young painters. Candace was a graduate student then, but—skinny, hair cropped—she looked like a boy, a shadowy street thief out of a foreign film. This was not entirely an achieved effect. After classes, Candace worked in a theater, selling tickets to movies she could not afford to see; then hurried home to paint for most of the night. Half of her meals in those days consisted of the leftover movie popcorn. She lived in a basement room rented from a bus driver and his older sister. During her last semester of graduate school—just before the photo had been snapped—Candace had to be hospitalized for three weeks; some toxicity developed from her living in the same room in which she painted. Not long after, however— thanks to the *Register* article and a professor who got his gallery to take Candace on—she started selling her work. She moved herself to that tiny house on the edge of Iowa City where, late one afternoon, Carson and Dana O'Connor and their son, Josh, stopped to buy the extra tomatoes and peppers that Candace had put out for sale on a sheet by the road.

The perfect family: handsome high-school-age son; imposing but doting dad; sleek wife with little blue pom-poms bobbling above the heels of her tennis shoes. The boy was the one who asked if they might come onto the porch to see what Candace was painting. Then the father—soon to become Carson—remembered the article from the

Register. He had admired the newspaper's photograph of her painting. The occasion shifted from a vegetable sale to the possibility of an actual painting purchase. Candace knew that she must focus on the painting sale, but something odd had begun to happen. Even while Carson and Dana O'Connor wandered about the shadowy little rooms behind the porch, and looked at the paintings propped here and there, and Candace gave Josh O'Connor a sketch that he admired, and told him which art teachers she could recommend at the university . . . all the while, she was aware of Carson. Though no one else seemed to notice, she understood that he was a glacier, slowly moving through her house, disturbing every single thing in his path, including her. When Carson and Dana O'Connor were ready to go—*well, they would surely keep that one she was working on in mind!*—Josh showed his parents the sketch that Candace had given him, and then Carson said that they ought to give Candace a gift, too, *come on.* She walked with them to their car, where Carson took from the trunk a pie-size hunk of brown, sugary rock.

"From the Burlington Pits," he explained. He moved a big finger over the sandy surface, pointing out the broken stems of crinoids, and it was all Candace could do, in spite of the presence of his wife and son, to keep from leaning into him. *Leaning.*

Am I crazy? she thought, after they drove off. Did something happen between us?

Very early in life, Candace had pulled in her borders, become the wick on a candle that burned only for her work. That she was a real painter, she had no doubt; it was her grounding as a human being that she questioned.

That man was *old,* she told herself as she went out to the wild garden at the back of the little house in order to pick a tomato for her own dinner. Hadn't he worn the same sort of ugly, white, short-sleeved shirts that her grandfather wore in hot weather—the fabric almost transparent, like the stuff of handkerchiefs?

Still, she was watching the road when he returned that evening.

He stood at the base of the steps leading to her porch. He was somber and silent, like someone on a rescue mission, a crusade. Candace said, "So, you want more vegetables?"

She was nervous enough that when he did not answer, she pretended he had, and he followed her when she came down the steps and walked toward the garden. There, in the dusk, the basswoods and oaks and maples that surrounded the little yard seemed to grow as thick as walls. Candace knew he stood close behind her as she lifted the big, prickly leaves of the zucchini plants. She wanted him to touch her—to somehow lay his hands on her. When he did, both hands on the tops of both of her bare arms, she leaned back against him, and the light cloth of his shirt, and she whispered, "Oh, my."

He held her as if she did not weigh anything at all, and she felt as if she might actually turn into something new, she was metamorphosing—but then he moaned an apology. He set her back on her feet and hurried to his car and drove away into the falling dark.

She hated him then.

A few mornings later, when his car pulled into her drive, she dashed down into the musty little cellar and hid. Until that time, she had allowed only one sweetheart into her life, a leather-jacketed poet she had met as an undergraduate. The very first time that Candace and the poet had quarreled, he had knocked out both of his front teeth with a big rock; that gesture, and the way its results complimented his slam-dancing persona, had left Candace with the sort of suspicions that were sure to ruin not just the romance in question but those that followed. Still, when Carson O'Connor stopped knocking, she hurried up the cellar stairs. Such relief: to find him sitting on the porch steps.

She did not trust in what was happening, but a few days later, when she caught a glimpse of the two of them in the squares of marbleized mirror a past tenant had glued to the bedroom door, she could not help but feel sympathetic toward their alliance. She and Carson O'Connor looked odd as the doll couple she had made do with as a kid: a skinny fashion doll swiped from a classmate's backpack, plus the husky toddler doll to whom ten-year-old Candy—Candace's true, tacky name, the one she had tried so hard to abandon—that toddler doll to whom ten-year-old Candy had given a felt-pen mustache so that he might better fit the part as he ground away at the fashion doll.

The fashion doll thievery had occurred in the spring of Candy's fifth-grade year. The following October, an early snow had fallen, and Morley Cleeve found the doll where Candy kept it hidden in a boot. Candy was whipped, the fashion doll burned, but neither Morley nor Georgine Cleeve could stop the fashion doll's lover from grieving and building monuments to his lost love, and had either Georgine or Morley climbed the apple tree behind the farm's empty chicken coop, they would have seen that the outline of a grand if irregular heart had been trampled into the snow in the field beyond.

III

Candace's current subject matter included a clipped hedge of pyracantha, three long-handled blue swimming pool tools tipped up against that hedge, and the blue-blue pool itself—all depicted on a stretched canvas whose dimensions measured exactly two inches smaller than the sliding glass doors of the room in which it stood (Candace's studio: red-brick walls, green indoor-outdoor carpet splotched and stiffened with the occasional smear of oil paint).

Down the little hallway lined with stretcher bars and rolls of canvas, here came Candace and Phoulish Phlame. With Phoulish Phlame riding on her head, Candace felt like a fanciful ship, richly if precariously appointed. It was pleasant in the studio, the odor of the cooler's damp excelsior pads mixing sweetly with the odors of turps and oils.

She eyed the bare curtain rod where she usually set the bird if she had to step outside. The bird always protested noisily at being left behind and Candace needed to go outside now to make sure that, overnight, no neighborhood cats or kids had sneaked into the backyard and moved the swimming pool tools off the duct-tape markers she had established before beginning the painting. Candace herself always disliked having to leave Phoulish Phlame inside. After all, Phoul had safely ventured outside with Candace on numerous occasions when Candace forgot the bird sat perched on her shoulder or head and realized her error only when the noise of Phoul's preening startled her or Carson called out a window, "Candy! You've got the bird with you!"

Carson did not feel much affection for Phoulish Phlame. Carson believed Candace used her relationship with the bird as a substitute for relationships with people. Also, the cockatiel had a tendency to hiss at Carson, and even bite, should Carson draw near his wife while the bird perched on her shoulder. Still, if he had seen her now, knowingly stepping outside with the bird, Carson would have chastised Candace for taking such a risk with something she loved so.

And he would have been right. The book that Candace had studied warned:

> Most pet bird deaths are the result of accidental release. The startled bird flies off when a cage is dropped on a trip to the vet, or when a visitor to the home unwittingly leaves a door open. Though your bird may be loving as any dog or cat, it will not know your neighborhood in such a way that it might return to the home. Startled by freedom, with no sense of its whereabouts, your bird will almost always take wing and become lost with neither food, water, nor cover.

Carefully, Candace skirted one of the long crisp strips of eucalyptus bark that lay scattered across the patio bricks—just the sort of thing that could release a snap that would make the bird start.

"Sweet thing," Candace murmured. "Careful now."

Zip. The cockatiel made a pleasant little noise as she drew a long tail feather through her bill. Zip.

The duct-tape guides had begun to curl in the heat on the bricks but the tools were in place, undisturbed.

"Golgotha," Carson called the painting, because of its grouping of three tools, but Golgotha was an echo from Carson's own Catholic youth. Candace saw the piece as a meditation on stillness, an attempt to achieve calm. Candace saw no point in inhabiting her paintings with symbols when every object shimmered with its own essence. This, of course, was a view that did not appeal to all audiences. A few months before, she had shipped a small canvas from the series of pool paintings to her parents, who returned it without a word. "Guess you wanted us to see you had a pool," Georgine Cleeve said when Candace telephoned for an explanation. "Well, now we know."

And what if there were some truth in what her mother said? Twenty-three swimming pool paintings, and who knew how many drawings, all of which she had conceived of as being pure in intention, and maybe she was just showing off? She would have laughed at the farm's response had it not seemed to diminish the possibility of art transmitting mystery, and suggested, instead, that every gesture might be a simple excrescence of vanity.

~

A melancholy day of painting. Some of the melancholy came from the departure of Carson, and yesterday's quarrel, but, late in the afternoon, when Candace mentally followed the gloom's trail—a little silvery slime, like that left behind by a slug—she wound up back at Carson's desk: the photographs of the soldier and the suicide. Perhaps they and Carson had somehow—with the permission of her unconscious, one supposed—managed to transform her painting into Carson's "Golgotha"? Or an inversion of the same? Though she was not quite sure what had happened, after six hours of work, the sky now looked lurid; the water in the swimming pool, dark and oily, as if a rotting body might pop to its surface at any moment.

"Wake up, I have something to show you."

Did the suicide actually say such a thing? Candace wondered. Or were those words just something that foamed up in the agitation surrounding his death? Were they some sort of slough that corresponded precisely to people's sense that the moment would remain in the witnessing girlfriend's brain forever?

Of course, if the words *were* the words of the suicide, they had to have come from the girlfriend.

Did she repeat them only once, to the police? Or had she, in grief and shock—and maybe even fury—said them over and over, to anyone who would listen?

Morosely, Candace looked up at the bird, now perched on its bare curtain rod. "Sewercide," Candace mumbled. There was some doggerel when Candace was a kid—a person who died with his head in a toilet? The last line a cantering bit about how the coroner came "and pronounced it 'sewercide'"?

As neither Candace nor the bird had left the studio since their trip to the patio that morning, Candace headed to the bathroom to fetch them a cup of water. The bird protested. She caught up with Candace in the hall and alighted on her shoulder.

After each sip of water, Phoulish Phlame gave a whistle. When the bird wanted no more, Candace set down the cup and worked a careful fingernail through the feathers on the bird's little skull and twig of neck. The bird turned her head this way and that, eyes closed in bliss. A sweet and wonderful thing: to give another being that sort of contentment. In response, Candace made her own noise of satisfaction, and, ever so lightly, drew her chin across the warm top of the bird's head.

She continued to draw her chin across the bird's head as she slid open the door to the patio once again. The heat of the desert afternoon hit her like a blast. One hundred and ten? Surely above one hundred and five? She wriggled into the rubber thongs she kept outside the door for those hours when the bricks were not negotiable in bare feet. Flop, flop, flop. She made her way to the swimming pool tools, and, this time, extracted from the trio the long-handled brush meant for removing the pool's algae. "Phoul," she murmured, "good girl. Aren't you a good girl?"

The trick with the algae brush was to push smoothly. One

smooth stroke down, move a step; another smooth stroke down. A little like painting a ceiling, or poling yourself down a river. A little like being a monk, maybe? Being a part of a world that required attention only to this task, and that deemed love and strife illusions? That would be a world in which to be *disillusioned* would be a fine thing, indeed.

"Mrs. O'Connor? Candy?"

Candace turned as a large young woman in black stepped out from behind an ailing hedge of mock oranges.

"Oh, it's your bird!" the woman cried exuberantly.

"Stop! Phoul!" Candace called, but too late. With a squawk, the bird lifted off, spun dizzily up and up—

"Where's it going?" The woman smiled, following the flight; then, after a look back at Candace, she cried, "Oh, my god! It's not supposed to do that, is it? I can tell . . . your face!"

Up into the drooping branches of the great eucalyptus trees that bordered the east side of the yard, Candace wailed, "Phoul! Come back!" In response, the bird made kittenish noises of distress.

"I can't believe this is happening!" The woman in black lowered her face to the stack of books in her arms. "No one answered the doorbell so I just walked around. I'm so sorry!"

Candace turned. It was Joyce Burton, Candace realized. The suicide's girlfriend, Joyce Burton, had dyed her pretty silver hair a queer, flat black since the party at which Candace had met her. Perhaps a gesture of mourning? Candace said, "No, listen, this is my fault," and then, fighting back tears for both Joyce Burton and Phoulish Phlame, "I was so sorry to hear about your boyfriend."

Joyce Burton nodded. "Thanks."

Together, they stared up into the gray-green leaves of the eucalyptus. "Here, Phoul. Come on down, Phoul," Candace called, and tried to cheer herself with a fact: *In its native Australia, the cockatiel feeds on the many varieties of eucalyptus.*

"Come on down, Phoul," Joyce Burton called.

Candace wanted to stop Joyce Burton for fear the woman might scare the bird again; still, she did not want to appear to correct this suffering soul, and so she asked, "I wonder if you could go into the front of the house, Joyce. Over Carson's desk, there should be a pair of binoculars."

At a flurry of noise above them, both women looked up. Out from the eucalyptus trees flew Phoulish Phlame—screaming, flopping up and down like something on a string, while six or seven house sparrows proceeded to dive at her.

"Phoul!" Candace cried. "Here, honey!"

Again, the cockatiel disappeared into the trees, but her protests, and those of the sparrows, persisted.

"Oh, man." Joyce Burton lifted the pile of books in her arms onto her head and held them there. She wore a black suit with a green sheen that made Candace think of the feathers on a turkey vulture. Today, the rings on Joyce Burton's big fingers were a wild assortment. A few looked as if they came from biker shops. A few were the sort of sweet antiques—amethyst, topaz—that people sometimes inherited from a grandmother, while others appeared to have come from the reservations, from street fairs and gum-ball machines. Joyce Burton said, "I got some wine and stuff in my car? Left over from the picnic? You want me to get us a drink while I grab the binoculars?"

"Oh. Not for me, thanks," Candace said.

Joyce Burton had been inside the house for several minutes when the sparrows drove Phoulish Phlame out into the open once more. The flock continued to dive at the lone bird until, with shriek after shriek, she streamed off over the rooftops, grew darker and darker with distance, then disappeared altogether.

Was that that, then?

Candace squeezed the tops of her arms, tight. Holding myself together, she thought. She continued to watch the empty sky—waiting for a rewinding of the bird's flight, for a dark spot to emerge and grow lighter and lighter. She turned when she heard the studio door slide on its tracks.

Joyce Burton did not step through the door but remained where she stood, and it took Candace a moment to realize that her visitor was crying.

"It really is my fault, Joyce," Candace said, tears filling her own eyes. She went to Joyce Burton and put her arms around that large woman in a hug, then added the excuse that she knew she would offer to Carson: "I didn't realize she was on my shoulder when I went outside."

Joyce Burton smiled wanly, then stepped away to take a drink from the bottle of wine she held in her hand. "It's not your bird that made me cry. It's just . . . I saw Ricky's picture on Carson's desk."

"Oh. I'm sorry."

Joyce Burton took another swig from her bottle. "I didn't see any binoculars in there but I left Carson's books on the desk. They were books Ricky borrowed." Another swig. A squint up at the trees. The pale skin around Joyce Burton's eyes was checked like the porcelain of an old cup. An effect of grief, Candace wondered. And that quiver in Joyce Burton's face—was it a continuing vibration from the explosion of the shotgun shell?

"I like that painting you're doing." Joyce Burton jerked a thumb in the direction of the studio. "Wow."

"Oh, thanks. I've worried it may have gotten a little . . . histrionic."

"No, no. Sturm und Drang, that sort of thing's good in a still life. So did your bird fly out again or anything?"

Candace hated having to tell Joyce Burton that the sparrows had driven off Phoulish Phlame entirely, and so, afterward, she offered up all of the optimistic cockatiel facts she knew:

> With its hot days and cool nights, the climate of Tucson is almost identical to the climate of the cockatiel's native eastern Australia. Lost cockatiels often meet up with other lost cockatiels. Supposedly, in Tucson, there was actually a flock living in a park on Twenty-second Street!

Joyce Burton leaned forward and smiled. Candace could not help noting that Joyce Burton had taken a seat in one of the pair of rickety canvas director's chairs in which her dead boyfriend had sat the fall before. Now a significant chair. A significant patio. Every street on which Rick Haynes had traveled: significant. This felt like the beginning of a wonderful chain of thought, but then a fear welled up in her: Suppose Carson took the cockatiel's departure for a sign that Candace was a presence from which it was desirable to escape?

Joyce Burton laughed. "Hey, maybe your bird will hook up with that flock on Twenty-second." She raised her bottle of wine in a salute. "What if we liberated all the cockatiels in Tucson, Candy? Filled the trees with pretty little birds!"

A moment before, Candace might have been irritated by Joyce Burton's scenario, but, just now, she could only stare at that poor, slightly drunk soul and wonder what it meant to be Joyce Burton, the one to whom Rick Haynes preferred death.

〜

All glass, no frame, but still big and square and awkward: such was the hall mirror that the bird had always favored. Hard labor for Candace to remove the toggle bolts that held the sheet of glass to the wall, to carry it through the kitchen and study and, then, to the makeshift carport beyond. Carson would have advised Candace to ask a neighbor for help in setting the mirror on top of the carport roof. Carson seemed to know many neighbors. Though Candace often chatted with children she met while out walking, the only adult neighbor that she knew was Wendell Yelland from across the street and Wendell Yelland had to be at least eighty. Suppose she asked Mr. Yelland for help and he tried to take on too much of the task, he had a stroke or some awful fall? Or, he was not hurt, but believed that helping Candace once meant that he could come by the house anytime, forever after, to ask a favor or just chat?

The mirror made a terrible screeching noise as Candace pushed it up and over the edge of the carport's flat roof. It would be ruined. When Carson saw it, he would say, "Was that necessary?" Or maybe he wouldn't. Whatever good or awful thing that you could predict might turn out to be incorrect. In any case, Candace longed to talk to Carson. He would be angry about the loss of the bird, yes, but he would understand that she felt terrible. Even more important, until she talked to Carson, Candace would not be able to get rid of the words that she needed to say to him: *Oh, Carson, I'm so sorry I didn't go with you! It was probably because I was distracted, missing you, that I went outside without seeing she was on my shoulder!*

A lie, yes, but a lie that was not without its germ of truth.

Why didn't Carson miss her so much that he had no choice but to call her before he even reached Iowa? If he worried about her so much, why didn't he need to call to see if she had been murdered or fallen into the swimming pool and drowned? Candace would have called Carson before she planned to, of that she felt certain. Though she would have done her best *not* to ask Carson if he thought that all people considered killing themselves whenever one person did.

∽

Everything. That was what Candace believed that she wanted to know about Carson. She did not understand, however, that the everything that she wanted to know, she also wanted to be palatable. Not just palatable: *laudable.* Carson did know this. Off and on, all night, as he drove through New Mexico and, then, Texas, headlights bleaching the scrub, sending long-eared jack rabbits off on a run, Carson thought with both tenderness and ire of how Candace—whom he surely loved as much as any man could love a woman—how Candace wanted for him to make his whole self up out of things that she could bear to know; how this was her way of helping him to become her private saint.

∽

When Carson and Candace had first moved to Tucson, Candace immediately set about stripping the ranch-style's walls. The home had been owned by only one family for the forty years that it had existed, and the built-up layers of paint and paper recorded changes in taste that Candace found fascinating. Originally, the owners had favored bold industrial colors—steel gray, crayon red, lime green. In what Candace supposed were the sixties or seventies, the family's palette had switched to yellow and orange, and a wild daisy print had gone up in the dining room and kitchen. Toward the end, as if nostalgic for an earlier, more eastern America, the family had hung "colonial" wallpapers in dusty blues and greens, and light fixtures with British pretensions. One of the latter, a "carriage lamp" affair, remained tipsily affixed to a post in the front yard, and after Candace had set the mirror and bird food and a bowl of water on the carport roof, and wandered the neighborhood crying up into the trees, and called the newspaper's Lost and Found and the Humane Society and the animal shelter, she hauled one of the backyard's director's chairs out front, and she spent what remained of the evening seated in the carriage lamp's little pool of yellow light.

In deference to the observatories perched on the outlying mountaintops, the city's rules on lighting left its nights much darker than the nights of most cities its size. There were no street lights at all on Candace and Carson's street, and though only rarely did cars travel the road, Candace could not help feeling conspicuous, on display, particularly when—just in case, every few minutes—she called up into the sky, "Phoul! Phoul!"

When not calling up into the trees, Candace read *Frankenstein*, which she found alternatingly boring and fascinating. She was dog-earing the page on which the monster says to Frankenstein, "You are my creator, but I am your Master," when old Wendell Yelland called a *halloo* from out of the dark, then slowly materialized: first, the white shirt; then the bald head and pale suede shoes.

"Took advantage of its opportunity to escape, huh?" Mr. Yelland said when Candace told him of the loss of the bird.

She did her best to smile. She went on to tell Mr. Yelland about Carson's trip to the Midwest. She knew Mr. Yelland would be interested, as he originally had come from Illinois. Mr. Yelland liked to explain that he had moved to Arizona for his allergies and asthma many years ago: "Back before everybody brought all the crap down here that gave them allergies up there!" Mr. Yelland always made it clear to Candace that he had been a "gay blade" as a young man in Illinois. "Though not what they mean by 'gay' now; those people ruined a perfectly good word, if you ask me."

Tonight, as Mr. Yelland talked, Candace glanced across the street now and then. The Yelland living room's curtains were drawn, and a soft yellow light came through them. Mr. Yelland's wife, Marie, would be over there, doing her treadmill, perhaps, while she watched television. Something was wrong with the Yelland marriage, Candace felt certain. Until the day that a middle-aged woman had stepped across the street to introduce herself to Candace as the visiting *daughter* of Wendell and Marie, Candace had mistaken that pair for sour brother and sister, forced to share a home for reasons of economy.

"Whenever me and my buddy got the chance, we rode the train into the city." The blooms of the acacia bothered Mr. Yelland during this part of the year, and he coughed and excused himself as he laughed into his handkerchief. "My buddy, Milt, was a little guy, but quite a dancer, and, believe it or not, I was a pretty good-looking fella back then, so we never lacked for fun. You could get into Chicago any hour and still find something to do. This night I'm thinking of, it was about eleven, and we'd taken our bags up to our hotel room, to clean up, you understand. We were staying at the Hilton. That was a pretty swank spot in those days, and when we got on the elevator to go out on the town, by god, there's Ava Gardner on the elevator with us! I poked Milt because I knew right off who she was, and she saw me see her, and she smiles and she says, 'Say, you boys wouldn't know where a person could get a steak at this hour, would you?' and, by god, if we didn't end up taking Ava Gardner out for a steak dinner!"

Candace hated to have to admit to Mr. Yelland that she did not know the identity of Ava Gardner because, clearly, the news disappointed him. "You watch *The Barefoot Contessa* one of these nights,"

Mr. Yelland said. "Beautiful woman!" He reached his chubby, furrowed hands into the light from the carriage lamp and he struck an imaginary match to show Candace exactly how Ava Gardner had lit his cigarette for him fifty years ago. "And never once took her eyes off mine!" he said. "*That* was star quality."

IV

At ten o'clock, Candace went inside the house and drew twenty cockatiel posters: bright, jaunty, sure to catch the eye. In the morning, under an odd, oyster-colored sky, she tacked the posters about the neighborhood—hopes rising and falling, again and again as, out of the corner of her eye, she mistook for Phoulish Phlame: a narrow-tailed mourning dove that sat on a telephone wire, a distant airplane, a wood bee, and a butterfly that zoomed in close.

"Phoul! Here, Phoul!"

Few names could have sounded more desperate or dumb, but, away from the boulevard, Candace had no audience. That neighborhood of brick ranch-styles sat quiet during the day. The only sounds to be heard were the low hum of air conditioners and swamp cooler motors, passing jets, traffic on the boulevard, the calls and chatter of the various wild birds: sparrows and Gila woodpeckers, verdins and house finches and doves.

The telephone began to ring as Candace let herself into the house once more: Joyce Burton, wanting to know if Candace's bird had come back.

As patiently as possible, Candace explained. "It can't actually come *back,* you see, because it doesn't know where I live."

"But, listen," said Joyce Burton, "I looked to see if you had an ad in the paper yet, and there was another person who'd lost a white cockatiel, so I called her—her name's Maryvonne. I gave her your number and told her I'd have you call—you know, in case either of you found the other one's bird or something?"

Candace wanted to object: *What business did Joyce Burton have telling people that Candace would telephone them?* Still, how could you chew out a woman who had witnessed the death of her sweetheart the week before? You couldn't, and so, with a sigh, Candace took down the number of this Maryvonne.

Maryvonne was at work at a place she identified as Deep Freeze when she answered Candace's call. Immediately, Maryvonne asked— in the sort of depressed Brooklyn accent that Candace associated with "comic" ads for products promising relief from heartburn or diarrhea—"So was your bird a young bird?" *Boid.* "My bird was young. I'm worrying somebody might call you about my bird and you'd keep him, you know?"

Candace's cheeks flushed at such bluntness, and with uncharacteristic aggression, she responded, "I guess I should worry about the same thing happening with you and *my* bird!"

"But I been trying to find mine three weeks now!" Maryvonne protested. "In all sincerity, if I don't find my bird, I think I'm gonna have to kill myself."

"Do you mean that?" Candace glanced down to the top of Carson's desk, the photo of grinning Rick Haynes. "Because when somebody says something like that, you're supposed to take it seriously."

"Forget it," Maryvonne said. She was just *down,* she said. Because of the bird. Her shitty job. Still, she seemed offended that Candace did not know the Deep Freeze. "It *is* the best place in town to get a smoothie." She sighed. "Anyways, my boss is going to fire me if I go check another bird sighting. You know how many cockatiels are lost in Tucson right now? Six, last I counted." Here, Maryvonne raised her voice to cry out to someone at Deep Freeze, "I know you're listening to me, Bruce! You laugh, but I know you're listening!"

How old was Maryvonne, Candace wondered. Nineteen? Fifty? In an effort to cheer the woman, Candace offered up her litany of optimistic cockatiel facts. To which Maryvonne responded that their white hybrids were in particular danger, even if they did find a flock; in the wild, Maryvonne explained, the flocks were made up of *gray* birds. "'Cause they all look alike, that gives them protection, see, since the enemy has a hard time keeping track of which bird he wants to catch—"

Alarmed by such news, and the possibility of worse to come, Candace interrupted, "We should probably get off, though. In case someone's trying to call us."

"You don't have a message machine?" Maryvonne snorted. "You wait. Since I lost my bird, I got it all. Caller ID, Call Transfer. You name it. And, hey, I got a recording of cockatiels you could try. You can borrow it this morning while I'm working—if you don't mind driving over here."

"Oh." Candace shivered—intrigued, alarmed. What if it turned out that Maryvonne was wonderful and the two became the best of friends? Or Maryvonne was totally insane and could not be gotten rid of ever? Or Candace liked Maryvonne but Carson did not? "Well, thanks, but I think I'll see if anyone calls first."

"Just a *minute*," Maryvonne snapped, then added, "not *you*, what's your name . . . Candace. Not you. I was talking to Bruce, here. Anyway, what bothers me—I'd feel better if I thought my bird *wanted* to go. That's what people think, you know, like, all along, he was just *dying* to escape from me."

"I know," Candace said. "I know. You sure you're okay, though? About what you said earlier? About killing yourself?"

"Yeah, yeah."

After Candace hung up the phone, she gave a yank on the middle drawer of Carson's desk. She meant to put the Rick Haynes flyer out of sight. The drawer, however, old and rarely used by Carson because of its crotchety ways, tipped forward and its small store of odds and ends spilled on the study floor. Candace was still picking up pens and clips when the telephone rang again.

Carson?

Maryvonne. Maryvonne had just received a telephone call from the receptionist at Valley National Bank! "A white cockatiel's sitting over their entrance! Can you get over there, 'cause Bruce'll kill me if I leave?"

Candace knew Valley National. A white mosquelike bank. Not too far off. Two miles? "Wait for me, Phoul," she murmured as she ran out to the curb and the ancient Buick Electra that had been a hand-me-down from Carson's parents. To Candace's relief, the thing started on the second try and, then, there was actually some pleasure—or stimulation, at any rate—in being a maniac on a rescue mission.

She was already parking the car in the bank lot when she realized she had failed to bring the bird's cage. A rather serious error, but one without consequences: the bird was not Phoulish Phlame. Candace knew this as soon as she stepped from the car and heard the cries. Before that moment, she would not have known that she knew the particular sound of her bird's voice. Even so, the cries of that strange bird on the thin ledge above the bank's gloomy tinted glass door stirred her, much the way the cries of any baby would have stirred her. Poor thing. Candace could see why it had chosen the spot over the door. There, it was high off the ground, and the smoked-glass windows made a mirror that convinced the bird it was not alone.

"Phoul," Candace called, in order to assert to those customers passing in and out the bank's door that she had a relationship to the bird, had a reason to be there. Some of the customers ignored Candace. Some smiled. Some looked up at the bird and shook their heads as if annoyed. A man with a purple yarmulke bobby-pinned to his fine net of hair stopped and asked, "How'd you lose it?" and Candace felt obliged to explain that the bird was not really her own bird, though her own bird *was* lost, and then—as if irritated or maybe just bored by the conversation—the bird over the door flew off with a squawk to a stand of eucalyptus across the street. "Excuse me," Candace said to the man in the yarmulke and hurried into the bank.

The receptionist had apparently been watching through the window and she stood right up from her desk. A friendly woman, Candace could tell. A little old-fashioned and wearing a cardigan against the bank's deep air-conditioning. "Was it your bird?" she asked Candace.

No, but did the receptionist still have the number of the woman she had spoken to earlier? The woman from the newspaper? Maryvonne?

"Oh, hell," said Maryvonne when Candace finished her update. "I got to quit this job. And don't make that face at me, Bruce! I'm going to take my tape over by that bank and see if it's my bird!"

Hand over the telephone's mouthpiece, Candace smiled at the waiting receptionist and whispered, "She's coming," then said into the telephone, "So, good luck, Maryvonne."

"You're not going to wait?" Maryvonne sounded hurt and a little angry. "What if it's your bird?"

"It's not my bird. I knew, right off," Candace said, but could tell that in her eagerness to get off the telephone, she sounded as if she lied.

~

That evening, the story that Candace relayed to Carson about the loss of the bird seemed to go by much too quickly and the pressure she had felt to speak to him was not relieved. While Carson said words of comfort, she stared at her reflection in the night-backed window over his desk, and she took some satisfaction in the fact that she had *not* drawn the shades.

Could it be that Carson's rules drove her to careless rebellion? That some lunatic was now able to look in at Candace, all alone in the house, because she kept up the blinds in revolt? But that wasn't the whole story. She *had* to keep the blinds raised so that if, by some wild chance, Phoulish Phlame should fly by, she could look in and see Candace through the glass. Stop. Announce that she was home.

"You called the newspaper?"

"It'll be in tomorrow. And I called the Humane Society and the *Shopper*."

"You know to be extra careful about talking to strangers on the phone?" A statement that was also a question. "Some nut could see your notice."

Adult voices drifted across the telephone line. A scraping of chairs. Laughter. Carson was staying with a former colleague and her husband, people with whom Carson and his ex-wife had been friends. Tomorrow, Carson explained, he and his kids might drive to the hog farm; then they would take a couple of rooms at a motel on the edge of Iowa City, a place where they could eat and swim and just loll around. When Carson said the name of the motel, Candace flushed. Before she knew Carson, while she was still an undergraduate, Candace had been at that motel with a man she met while working at the movie theater. The man came from Pennsylvania and had a connection to the big college testing company down the road from the motel. Danny Halverson. Danny Halverson took Candace out for dinner at the motel's restaurant, a big beef and whiskey sort of place with plaid banquettes. Afterward, when Danny Halverson suggested they stop by his room for a drink, Candace thought it would be unsophisticated to object. Of course, she *was* unsophisticated. Downright *dumb*, she later realized—though she had been to the dorm rooms of a few boys by then. The boys, like the other people in her classes, assumed she was like them. They did not know she found the university a foreign country. She had kissed a few of those boys. She did not object when plump but handsome Danny Halverson kissed her. A grownup wearing a three-piece suit and an aftershave lotion that made her simultaneously want to laugh and swoon, Danny Halverson struck Candace as the visual equivalent of the restaurant below them. After he took off her shirt, however, Danny Halverson revealed that he had a camera in his room. He wanted to take pictures of Candace without her clothes. Though Danny Halverson's fleshy neck turned pink at the announcement of his desire, Candace found him sufficiently intimidating that she did allow him to snap one picture (bra, jeans, sneakers) before she announced a need to use the bathroom, and slipped out into the motel hall with a bath towel draped over her bare shoulders, and made her way to her room in the bus driver's house, first, by walking in the boggy ditches between the motel and town, then darting through backyards and alleys.

Carson said, "There's no reason you couldn't fly up here, Candy. If you're feeling too bad. You could drive on to Illinois with me."

"But I'm supposed to be *working*. And how could I leave, anyway, while I'm waiting to hear about Phoul?"

Carson sighed. "I suppose Joyce felt awful about it. How'd she seem to be doing, anyway?"

Candace did not mention Joyce Burton's drinking for fear she might be tattling. Which struck her as an accomplishment until she considered the possibility that perhaps she did not mention the drinking for fear it would make Carson even more concerned about Joyce Burton's state of mind.

Did Candace love Carson so because, by having to consider his mortality, she found her own, and, then, curled at its side—almost invisible, that embryo that had waited for a source of nourishment to come along—her morality?

As soon as the two hung up, Candace felt lonely, and she went to the refrigerator, where she had posted Maryvonne's telephone numbers.

"There wasn't any bird around when *I* got to Valley National! And am I in deep shit at work now!" said Maryvonne. "Oh, and that woman called again, you know? The one that scared off your bird in the first place? She's coming by to make a copy of my cockatiel tape. I guess she wants to find your bird. Is she weird? Like, do you think she'll screw up my tape?"

"Oh, no." For a moment, discretion stopped Candace from saying more; but then a sense that she ought to defend Joyce Burton arose in her, and she added, "She's been through a lot lately. You may have read in the paper—a student at the university killed himself last week? That was her boyfriend. I mean, he did it in front of her. The creep."

"I saw that! That was awful! So you know them, huh?"

"Just a little," Candace said, then sternly corrected herself, "Not really. He was my husband's student. My husband knew him. That's why she came by the house. To bring back books he'd borrowed from my husband."

Maryvonne made a loud shivering noise—ooooo! "So now you got books in your house some *dead* guy read. . . ."

The books sat on Carson's desk, among them a pamphlet on microfossils and a volume of *Philosophical Transactions of the Royal Society of London.*

"Talk about creepy newspaper stories, though!" Maryvonne made her shivering noise again. "Did you see that one about the scuba diver that died in the forest fire? Some place in California?"

Candace did not answer. She felt suddenly guilt stricken, hot. How could she have offered up Joyce Burton's sad story to a stranger? She was a monster!

"Stop me if you heard this," Maryvonne continued, "but, like, after this big forest fire in California, the Forest Service guys found a body in the ashes, and it was dressed in full *scuba gear,* and they're all, like, scratching their heads. 'How'd a guy in *scuba gear* end up in a fucking forest fire?' Then this investigator's reading his newspaper over breakfast, and he sees some local diver guy disappeared on a dive, and, oh, *shit,* he realizes what happened is, this guy, out diving, got scooped up by one of the big planes they use to take up ocean water to dump on *forest fires!"*

Was that story true? After Candace got off the telephone with Maryvonne, she told herself it was *not* true. It was probably one of those apocryphal tales, like the one in which the medical student goes to receive his cadaver, and it turns out to be his fiancée.

Still, that night, when Candace climbed into bed, the scuba diver story came back to her, and she could not stop herself from imagining the horror of being scooped up by a huge and noisy thing, trapped, absolutely trapped, and then falling from the sky into roaring flames. To distract herself from such imaginings, Candace tried to unravel the horrible fascination such stories held. With their freakish coincidences, their ironies, they were quite different from the sad story told by the Gulf War vet. The vet went about telling his story in an attempt to inspire others, and, perhaps, even himself; telling his story gave him a reason to live.

∽

The column numbered 16 in the Personals section of the *Arizona Daily Star* was the one for Lost and Found. Candace, reading the column while waiting for the kitchen timer to ding, remembered how reluctantly she had checked it in the weeks after Phoulish Phlame first flew down to her at the pool.

The kitchen timer was set to ring at nine o'clock, the hour at which the Humane Society would open, and Candace could give them a call.

Among the lost: a set of Snap-On tools, a conure named Petra, an aged basset hound needing medicine, a tennis bracelet, the cockatiels belonging to Maryvonne and Candace, a briefcase whose return would bring a reward, no questions asked.

Found: four mixed-breed puppies, a gray cockatiel, a set of bow and arrows, an elderly black Lab, a medieval-type costume (call to identify).

If no one claimed them, could Candace please have the puppies, the old black Lab, the gray cockatiel? She stared at the column, trying to make her yearning for Phoul form a concretion so dense its gravity would pull the bird home.

"Oh," said the friendly Humane Society worker who took Candace's call, "just a minute ago, when I pulled in, there was a guy in the parking lot with a white cockatiel, and while I opened up, the family that'd lost it pulled in!"

"But, how'd they know for sure it was their cockatiel?" Candace was panicky, her cheeks inflamed. "I mean, my cockatiel's white, too. And I have a friend who's got a white one, lost, too." At her use of the word "friend," Candace blushed. Such presumption! "Did you take their phone number or anything?" she asked hopefully.

"It was their bird, miss." The Humane Society woman was now firmly disapproving. "The children recognized it right off."

After the Humane Society woman hung up, Candace stared out at the blue-blue sky. Had it cooled off at all last night? Recently, she had read an article stating that, in Phoenix, the mushrooming buildings and streets now trapped so much of the desert heat that the city no longer experienced the relief of nighttime cooling. *In fast-growing*

Tucson and Phoenix, development moves into open land at the rate of one acre an hour. "Hey!" On the mirror upon the carport roof, house finches and sparrows and white-winged doves now devoured the seed she had put out for Phoulish Phlame. She pounded on the screen door until the birds flew off; then she picked up the telephone again.

Maryvonne proved gratifyingly distressed by the Humane Society story. "Did you give them our numbers?" she asked. "In case the people call back?"

"Yes." Candace looked out at the carport roof. The birds had descended on the seeds once more, but now they flew up as a small blue car parked in front of the old Buick.

An enormous basket began to emerge from the driver's side of the car. No, not a basket. One of the enormous sombreros that certain tourists picked up down in Nogales, but that no Mexicans actually wore anymore—if they had ever worn them at all.

The person beneath the sombrero began to approach the house. Joyce Burton. Who, spying Candace at the window, called out, "I got a cockatiel in my car!"

"Hold on," Candace told Maryvonne. "That woman's here who borrowed your tape and she's got a bird." Candace set down the telephone, though she could hear Maryvonne demand: "What color? Put her on!"

Joyce Burton was red-faced with excitement, so Candace did not feel at all embarrassed running across the gravel yard to the little blue car.

"By the back right—no, there it goes!"

The bird inside the car flew, shrieking, to cling to a window that Joyce Burton had left cracked open at the top.

"Phoul," Candace called. She could see that the bird's back was not entirely white but marked by asymmetrical blotches of yellow and gray, but for both her own and Joyce Burton's sake—perhaps this bird could turn into her bird?—she stayed with hands cupped against the window, staring in, until she had no choice but to turn to Joyce Burton and smile and shake her head.

Joyce Burton removed the sombrero and slapped it gloomily against her thigh. "How do you know for sure?"

"The markings, and she wouldn't act like that with me. But, hey!" Candace smiled. "It's amazing you *found* a bird, Joyce! And *caught* it! Come on and we'll tell Maryvonne. I think her bird's white like mine, but I bet she'll want to come see this one, just to make sure."

When the women entered the house, they found that Maryvonne's voice continued to buzz from the telephone on Carson's desk and, apparently meaning to enter into the spirit of things, Joyce Burton shouted from across the room a jolly, "Hey, Maryvonne!" When she picked up the receiver, however, Joyce Burton made a face of repugnance before she said in a normal voice, "Why don't you come over to Candy's and check out this bird?"

~

In the shade of the carport, while Joyce Burton and Candace waited for Maryvonne, Joyce Burton played her copy of Maryvonne's cockatiel tape and told Candace the details of her capture of the bird now squawking in her car. "They say you're not supposed to be timid at all, so as soon as the bird started eating the millet, I threw a blanket on it and *pounced*."

"I'm impressed," Candace said.

Joyce bowed, laughed, then went to the trunk of her little car and opened it and pulled two bottles of beer from a cooler there. "These are warm—more leftovers from the picnic—but you want one? Pretend we're British or something?"

Candace shook her head. It occurred to her that she might get closer to Joyce Burton by explaining that, actually, because of her father, she was afraid of drinking any sort of alcohol, period; instead, she said, "In a way, don't you think it's sort of sad these birds can be tricked so easily? I mean, it's great a lost bird will come down to the tape, but it seems sort of pathetic." She meant to go on to tell Joyce Burton that the term "stool pigeon" originated from the practice of tying a bird to a stool so that its calls might lure others of its kind into a net, but, over by the raised trunk of her car, Joyce Burton now appeared to be laughing—crying?—no, laughing, so Candace said, "Do you think it was smart for me to tell Maryvonne where I live? I mean, Carson would have a fit."

"*Carson?*" Joyce Burton made wide eyes.

Candace nodded. "He's a worrywart."

"How funny! I guess it makes sense, though, since he likes to take care of people and all." Joyce Burton smiled at Candace. "Everybody at school loves Carson, you know. Ricky practically idolized him. He would have liked to *be* Carson! You know those awful shirts Carson wears? Rick had started wearing those!"

Joyce Burton laughed, but Candace was not sure that meant that she should laugh. "Carson really liked Rick, too," she said.

Joyce Burton nodded. "That meant a lot to him. Once, last fall, I know they had a good talk and it helped Rick . . . for a while, anyway." She turned the ring on her index finger back and forth. The ring was so large and elaborate that bending the finger it adorned would have been an impossibility. "A lot of people liked Ricky because they thought he was crazy. You know: the wild man. I loved him for other reasons." Joyce Burton held the ring-studded hand out before herself and gave it a hard stare. "You know what he did?" she asked.

For a moment, Candace did not understand that Joyce Burton referred to Rick Haynes's suicide. She assumed that the question was rhetorical, and that Joyce Burton meant to offer an example of what had made her love Rick Haynes; but Joyce Burton continued, "He was really, really drunk. I mean, even though he talked about killing himself a lot, believe me, he'd be so fucking embarrassed if he knew he actually did it."

With a scrape, Mrs. Yelland from across the street dragged her green recycling bin to the curb. In case the old lady looked their way, Candace raised her hand to wave, then, lips trembling, she said, "I've thought about doing it, Joyce. Before I met Carson, I figured thinking about killing yourself was, like, a sign of mental health. Well, not mental *health*, maybe, but it showed a person had taken a realistic look at life. I know this sounds crazy, but *now* one of the main reasons I think about killing myself is because life's so short!" She gave a stuttering laugh, then tried to meet Joyce Burton's eyes to see if she had gone too far. When Joyce Burton did not look up from turning the rings on her fingers this way and that, Candace hurried on, "Because life's so short, I can't stand that, see? And . . . with Carson. I know I should change some things between us, but then I think, suppose I did. What if he didn't love me then, or I didn't love him either?"

~

Joyce Burton smiled at Carson's wife and nodded. Ever since Rick's suicide, people had been telling Joyce their disaster stories; not just stories of suicides, but—as if they intuitively understood the thin line between suicide and accident—a story of a little kid who drank drain cleaner, a stepbrother who died grabbing a rainspout electrified by faulty wiring. Car wrecks, drownings, sudden infant death syndrome, betrayal. Afterward, the storytellers sat back and waited. They seemed to expect Joyce to be wiser than she had been just a week ago. Of course, they were concerned about Joyce, and they missed Ricky, but they also seemed to believe that Joyce was a grand searchlight that could illuminate all the nooks and crannies of their troubled pasts. What was that all about? Maybe, during their own troubles, people had not been able to see the outlines well enough? Or maybe they were *missing* their troubles now? They wanted to go back and visit the sites of disaster? Feel something rock their bones?

Though this conversation with Carson's wife was a little different from her conversations with the others, Joyce believed that Carson's wife, too, had a story she wanted to tell.

But Joyce was wrong.

All that Candace had just then was a question that she knew Joyce Burton could not answer: Which was better, to be the one who goes or the one who stays behind?

V

An oddity: the taped cockatiel calls suddenly becoming a lush old ballad, already well under way, and offering up its own plaint of terrible longing, nostalgia.

Joyce Burton laughed. "I screwed up, there. I'd made my grandma a tape of old Nat King Cole—you know who he was?—and I didn't label it, and, well, I've been kind of fucked up lately, and somehow I copied Maryvonne's tape over the first thirty minutes of Nat King Cole."

"This has to be such a hard time for you," Candace said. She laid a shy hand on Joyce Burton's shoulder, then added, "I *can't* imagine." She knew from years of reading "Dear Abby" that you were not to say, "I *can* imagine," and she wanted to say the right thing, to offer sympathy without becoming the Emotion Hog, the Big Bore. Hard, she bit her lip. Dug the nails of her free hand into her palm.

"Nothing like a good hot beer." Joyce Burton's mouth moved this way and that. Maybe she would begin to cry now? And then Candace could cry with her?

No. Joyce Burton inserted her forearm under her strange black hair and lifted it, cooling her neck. She said, "When my grandpa was still alive, we used to go out to this steak house where they had a jukebox with oldies on it, and we'd always put Nat King Cole on the jukebox—this song, 'Stardust'—and my grandparents would dance, and everybody would watch them. I thought they were these great dancers just because they loved each other, but last week, when my parents were here for Ricky's funeral, my mom was talking about how my grandpa used to come home for lunch everyday, so he and my grandma could practice their steps." Joyce Burton made a face and sighed as if she found the story depressing.

"Well," said Candace in what she hoped was an encouraging—but not *smarmy*—sort of voice, "but that's nice, too."

"Maybe," Joyce Burton said, then pointed one of her ring-heavy hands to the street. There, a teal-colored van approached; then the van was skidding to a stop in front of the carport. "Here's Maryvonne,"

Joyce Burton said and, a moment later, a tall and willowy young woman in a white waitress uniform emerged from the van and rushed their way, birdcage rattling in her hand. "Hey, Maryvonne," Joyce Burton called, and held up her two bottles of beer, one of them now almost empty.

Candace could not put this Maryvonne together with the woman from the telephone until the voice of Maryvonne issued from the newcomer's mouth: "So, where's the bird? You Candace?"

Candace nodded, though Maryvonne was already at the window of Joyce Burton's car, looking in. "Oh, shit! That's not my bird!" she cried, then turned her head to another angle. "That bird's all puffed up and ugly!"

Joyce Burton laughed—a toot sounded across the mouth of her beer bottle—but Candace whispered, "Don't say that, Maryvonne. It's upset. Birds get puffy like that when they're upset."

Maryvonne rolled her eyes as she took a warm beer from Joyce Burton. "I don't know about your bird, Candy, but mine's little and pretty."

Candy. Had Maryvonne picked that up from Joyce Burton? Candace stared down the street to the point where the curbs gave way and the pale road and the gravel front yards blended one into the other. "I should call the Humane Society," she said. "Since that family might have taken the wrong bird—one of our birds—I should let the Humane Society know about this one. In case that family calls back."

"Hold your horses," said Maryvonne, "we're not calling anybody yet," and she slid herself and her cage into the backseat of Joyce Burton's car.

The distressed cockatiel flew, squawking, from driver's window to front passenger's window, while Maryvonne sat in the back of the car, drinking her bottle of warm beer. When the bird finally decided to cling to the driver's window, Maryvonne cracked open the window closest to herself and whispered to Candace and Joyce, "So what do you guys think? You think it could be my bird?"

"But wasn't your bird's back all white, too?" Candace asked.

Maryvonne rubbed at her eyes. "Is that what I told you?" she said around a large yawn.

Joyce Burton fetched a second bottle of beer for Maryvonne and fitted it and a bottle opener through the cracked window. "Have another beer while we give some thought to the matter," she said with a laugh.

"So, bird." Maryvonne leaned forward and rested her chin on the carseat. "Are you my bird or what?"

Then, halfway through the second beer—Joyce Burton had just finished her tale of the bird's capture—Maryvonne declared, "I thought I'd never see the little bugger again! How can I thank you, Joyce?"

Joyce Burton, too, had finished a second beer by then. She put the sombrero back on her head—"Nogales" spelled out across the crown in frayed neon green yarn. Joyce Burton danced around in a circle for Maryvonne and made yipping noises. Maryvonne laughed. Candace laughed but only to appear part of the group. In the midst of the other women's chumminess, Candace felt irremediably sober, and a little anxious. That grateful look on Maryvonne's face suggested to Candace that Maryvonne might, at any minute, blurt something to Joyce Burton about the fact that Candace had told her of Rick Haynes's suicide. Also, Candace longed to appear decisive, capable of action, and so she put her hand on the car door and said, "Scoot over, Maryvonne."

Maryvonne did as she was told. Then Candace slid into Joyce Burton's car and, with an efficiency that astonished even herself, caught up the pied cockatiel and inserted it in Maryvonne's cage.

$\sim$

She told herself that she was glad when the pair finally left. "Idiots," she muttered. Think of the poor person to whom the bird truly belonged! And poor Rick Haynes, now subject to Joyce Burton's inter-pretation of his death! When she reentered the house, she yanked from beneath its refrigerator magnet the sheet of paper that held Maryvonne's telephone numbers and she threw it in the trash.

Off and on, throughout the rest of the day, while she walked about the neighborhood, crying "Phoul, here Phoul," she sent a mental message to Carson: *Call me.* While she worked in her studio—trying to remove from her painting what appeared to be angry thunderclouds in the sky above the pool—*Call me.*

That night, from the carriage lantern's golden halo of light: *Call me.*

Sometimes, Candace did believe that she might, actually, have some sort of powers, be a kind of witch; still, she jerked in the director's chair when the telephone began to ring inside the house.

The caller, however, was not Carson, but a young man who said, "I think I've got your bird. It came down to me while I was mountain-biking. Up by Sabino?"

"What about the tail feathers?" Candace asked. She did not want to get her hopes up. "Does it have some reddish paint on the tail feathers?"

"Maybe. It was real friendly when it flew down to me," the caller said, "but now it doesn't want to be touched. It isn't eating or anything so I think it may be sick."

Sick. Candace's chest filled with a bright vapor that immediately rolled up behind her forehead, then down the back of her skull. Still, this time, she did remember to carry the cage out to the Buick. To tell herself, as she pulled on the lights and put the car in gear, *Calm down. Don't drive over some little kid in the street because you're not watching where you're going. Don't speed and get delayed by a cop.*

In the dark, in that dark town, it was often hard to read the street signs, let alone find an unfamiliar address, but she located the number without too much trouble. The house to which it belonged, however, looked uninhabited. A small white stucco bungalow. Run-down. A sickly ochre in the light from the sodium lamp at the intersection.

The big birdcage rattled and banged against her thigh as she made her way up the cracked sidewalk. Did the cage smell? As if she were a girl again, coming in from the sloppy hog farm, she worried she might be turned away for stinking.

The top half of the front door was made of glass, uncurtained. She could see inside the house, through a dark and cluttered room to a room beyond lit only by the blue glow of a television. There, a group of boys—nineteen, twenty years old—slouched on the floor and a broken couch. When she knocked, two barking dogs raced from some other part of the house and leapt up wildly against the rattling door. The boys watching the television glanced Candace's way, but made no move to let her inside.

"*Kurt!*" one of them finally called over the barking of the dogs. "*It's the bird lady!*"

A boy with a shaved head and unlaced boots appeared from some other part of the house and, eyes down, not looking at Candace at all, he came to the door and opened it. "Knock it off!" he said to the dogs, and then, to Candace, "Bird's upstairs." When he turned and began to walk deeper into the house, she followed. She had known boys in graduate school who looked like this boy and his roommates. Boys who appeared mentally ill, or as if mentally ill barbers had cut their hair. Sometimes they were nice. The poet who had knocked out his own front teeth with the rock had, after all, made an elaborate ceramic card for his mother on Mother's Day and volunteered once a week at a soup kitchen.

In the room that held the television-watchers, Kurt—like a boy sent to bed by his elders—sullenly began to make his way up a metal spiral staircase that looked as if it had been torn out of a prison and installed in the bungalow in order to up the air of depravity in the place.

"Excuse me," Candace said as she passed between the other boys and their TV show.

Of course, she felt preposterous, annoying, terrified. The spiral staircase rang with her tread. Perhaps she made it impossible for the boys to hear their television show. Perhaps the show was just a cover, anyway. Really, this was where you were killed. Where the crowd leapt upon you and, after torturing you for a good long time, tore you to bits. The end. *The end.*

At the top of the stairs, she tried to take courage from the fact that whoever had decorated the attic space had worked to make it cheerful with bright squares of carpet remnants and pillows.

Across the attic, the boy fiddled with a cage he appeared to have made of hog-fencing. Candace hurried to where he stood. The bird that perched on a twig inside the homemade cage was rumpled, shrunk inside its feathers like an ancient homeless person wrapped up in newspapers against the cold. *Phoul.*

"Phoul," Candace said.

The bird raised her head and gave a plaintive peep.

"Oh, honey," she sighed, "how're you doing?"

"It was real friendly when it came down to me," said the boy. Candace understood that he could not help sounding resentful, hurt, just as she could not help rambling while she took the bird from the cage and kissed her beak: "Yeah, she may be a little sick. Her nostrils are inflamed. And see this red paint on her feathers? That's the paint I was talking about. I'm a painter. That's alizarin crimson."

Tentatively, the boy reached out a hand to stroke the bird. She hissed at him in her old, ugly way—the way she hissed at Carson— and the boy said a bitter, "So I guess it's your bird, all right."

Candace felt sorry for the boy though he still scared her a bit. She could imagine how things had been. Frightened and hungry and exhausted, the bird had been docile. Perhaps she stayed on the boy's shoulder all the way back to town. She took a seed from his lips, nibbled the fine hairs at the back of his neck. But then she found herself stuck in a cage and began mourning. From the start, Candace had known not to confine the bird to a cage.

"I want to give you a check. A little reward." She glanced toward the stairs. From what she could gather, the boys below watched a show on public television. Something about the Orient Express, it seemed. Surely a pack of potential killers would not watch a show about the Orient Express. Still, as soon as she handed the boy the check, it occurred to her that Carson would be upset that she had, in effect, given her name and address to a boy who already had her phone number from the Lost and Found page. It was too late, however, to suggest she give him cash instead, and she inserted the bird in the cage, made her way down the noisy stairs, past the other boys, and out the door.

Is my husband here yet? She was on Grant Road, waiting at a red light when she realized *that* was what she ought to have said as soon as she reached the boys' house. *Is my husband here yet?* Oh, and she should have left a note at the house explaining where she had gone and why. What if she had been murdered and Carson just assumed she had run off? Periodically, bodies—male, female, hard to identify—showed up in the desert surrounding the city. Everything had turned out fine, yes, but she had not prepared for disaster. Suppose she had ended up dead when she did not mean to, and people imagined she had let herself get killed on purpose?

"He'd be so fucking embarrassed if he knew he actually did it."

Really, Joyce Burton herself had provided Candace an excellent reason to live, hadn't she: To delay, as long as possible, giving over your story to other people's interpretation.

VI

Calling Carson's motel in Iowa City made Candace feel shy. A little silly, nervous. Though she needed to tell him whom she loved best of her relief at the return of the bird—now curled up wearily in the crook of Candace's neck—Candace understood her news would matter to Carson only because he cared for her.

"I'm sorry it's so late, but I needed to let you know."

"Hey, I'm really happy for you," Carson said, and, then, as he moved to a phone in the adjoining room, he called out, "Hey, you guys, Candy found her bird."

She rested her cheek against the bird's head. One of the children would have hold of the phone now. Would he or she say hello? Apparently not. It seemed Josh believed that Carson and Candace had been involved with each other before the family stopped to buy vegetables; that Carson had tried to trick Josh into liking Candace before he knew the truth of who she was.

"We're watching a movie," Carson said. Was that click of the other receiver being returned to the cradle a genuine click? A fake click? She felt too disarmed to respond appropriately when Carson added, "I wish you were here."

The three of them had made the trip to the hog farm that morning, Carson reported. Candace's mother had taken them on a tour and made them lunch.

"Where was my dad?"

"He wasn't feeling so good, I guess. We didn't see him." After a moment's pause, Carson said, "Hey, it was fine, Candy. But I *did* have a hard time convincing Georgine that the kids couldn't take home a piglet!" He laughed. "She was funny. She liked the kids, I think. They were good. They asked a lot of questions."

Candace let Carson continue to draw his cozy picture of the visit. Though she could only imagine her dark little mother dragging herself through the visit, and her father knocking up against the furniture in the bedroom, why not allow Carson's version to stand?

"But I should let you go back to your movie," Candace said. She knew how bored she sounded. Bored, detached.

"You're my girl, though, right?" Carson asked.

"Right."

After she hung up, Candace looked in the trash can for Maryvonne's home telephone number. She wanted to tell Maryvonne about Phoul; to hear what Maryvonne now had to say about the pied bird caught by Joyce Burton. Maybe Maryvonne had decided to call the paper or the Humane Society to report the pied bird found. Maybe Candace could tell Maryvonne about how Carson had taken his children to visit the farm and made that godawful place sound just fine.

Candace knew perfectly well, however, that Maryvonne's number had gone with the garbage and recycling that she had put out after Maryvonne and Joyce Burton left that afternoon.

Three-two-five? Three-two-seven? The numbers together were a flock, so similar it was difficult to distinguish one from the other, and after disturbing several households, Candace gave up trying.

She *did* find the number for the Deep Freeze in the directory. According to the message machine, the Deep Freeze would open at nine in the morning. The special on banana-malt power shakes would last until the end of the month.

~

In the morning, however, Candace did not call Maryvonne at the Deep Freeze. The truth: Candace felt slightly bitter. Now that Maryvonne had a cockatiel in her possession, apparently she did not care about the fate of Candace's bird.

Phoulish Phlame complained from inside the screen door, while outside—the gravel yard already hot from the climbing sun— Candace dragged the director's chair from its spot by the carriage lamp to the carport. A stepladder would have been preferable to the director's chair, she supposed, but surely the worst she could do in a fall from the chair was to break a leg or an arm, and no one could construe either injury as the result of suicidal impulses.

Carefully—like an acrobat getting ready for a stunt—she clutched the chair's arms, then placed a foot on each of the side supports of the chair's canvas seat; and only after she felt steady in that squat did she attempt to stand.

One swaying moment—then a gasp—before her ribs crashed into the edge of the roof. But she was okay. Okay. She steadied herself, then looked at the mirror. Just as she had suspected, it was ruined, the silvering shoved back in long terrible ribbons, like charred skin. But there was something beautiful in the total effect: through the scrapes in the glass, she could see—like the perfect undisturbed sediment at the bottom of a still pond—a dense layer of eucalyptus pods and old leaves, and, here and there a feather, a bright strand of live cat's-claw vine; and all of this contained by a sweet reflection of overhead clouds and trees.

A perfect composition, she thought, but not hers, and she set to working the mirror close enough to the lip of the roof that she would be able to grasp its edges once she stood on the ground again.

When she was finally down, she moved the director's chair out of the way, and began to pull the mirror toward herself. More scraping sounded. With some effort, slowly backing away from the carport, she drew the edge of the heavy pane onto the top of her chest, then eased the weight onto breasts, down to stomach and the tops of thighs, before making a last painful adjustment and, with hobbled step, moving the mirror back through the screen door and into the house.

With a yelp, she set the mirror on top of Carson's desk. There, her weary self was reflected, and then, a flutter of wings as Phoul instantly flew to Candace's head, landed, peeked over that cliff to see what she could see: bill, small white face, bright eyes. The flyer for the suicide's picnic was visible through the scrapes in the mirror. The still intact silvering—now reflecting the ceiling—hid the suicide's face, but his shirt was visible: a turquoise shirt covered with bright tropical birds, and, below this, *Rick Haynes, 1969–1997.*

Candace did not feel angry with Rick Haynes anymore. Though his suicide had been at least partially an act of aggression, who was she to say it had not been an intimate thing, too? Maybe Rick Haynes was capable of being more intimate with another person than she was. Maybe, in killing himself in front of Joyce Burton, he had meant, in his own way, to marry himself to her forever. In another world, that is. A world where suicide expressed the keenest desire to exist, a world where the suicide now lived—like a glove turned inside out and worn on the opposite hand.

Candace could understand that.

Candace supposed she really ought to call Joyce Burton. Tell her about finding the bird. Though this would mean that, later, when Candace was unable to stop herself from telling Carson of the call, he would say, "Good for you! I'm proud of you, Candy! I bet Joyce can use all the friends she can get these days, and I wouldn't be at all surprised to find the two of you have a lot in common!"

Burton, Joyce did not appear in the telephone directory. Candace hesitated before turning the pages of the big slippery book to *Haynes, Rick.* Using the dead man as an avenue to Joyce Burton—would it be somehow disrespectful? she wondered. Too utilitarian? Or—a more primitive bell chimed in her head—would it somehow bring her uncomfortably close to Haynes in the world of the dead?

But that was silly. Babyish. You had to be brave.

She flipped the pages and found the name quickly in its spot in an upper-right-hand corner. *Haynes, Rick.*

Suppose someone did not know the owner of that name was dead, and not just dead but dead by his own hand, his death his own creation. To such a person, the name would appear no different from any of the other names that followed it in the column—a Scott and a Sean and a Sharon—but Candace knew that *Haynes, Rick* had been transformed to something magical, mysterious: an artifact if not a piece of art.

Significant.

She smoothed her finger over the directory page, the tiny letters and numerals of the name, address, telephone number; then, while she let the telephone ring for Joyce Burton, she carefully tore the page from the directory and she folded it into a square that she placed in her pocket, meaning to save it just as she would have saved any letter that had been meant especially for her.